Mel Bay Presents
Tárrega in Tablature
By Ben Bolt

with text
in English, Spanish,
French and Japanese

CD CONTENTS

1	Prelude in E [:42]	14	Prelude in A Minor [1:02]
2	Prelude in A Minor [:34]	15	Prelude [1:15]
3	Lágrima [1:12]	16	Prelude [1:13]
4	Prelude in G Major [:46]	17	Prelude in A Major [:20]
5	Prelude in D Major [:24]	18	Danza Mora [1:52]
6	Prelude in D [:34]	19	Marieta! [1:45]
7	Prelude (Endecha) [:32]	20	Mazurca En Sol [2:20]
8	Prelude (Lento) [:32]	21	Maria [2:00]
9	Prelude (Moderato) [1:16]	22	Minuetto [1:56]
10	Prelude in D Minor [:32]	23	Adelita [:54]
11	Prelude [:53]	24	Pavana [1:17]
12	Prelude [:56]	25	Capricho Arabe [4:45]
13	Prelude in A [:52]		

1 2 3 4 5 6 7 8 9 0

Visit us on the Web at www.melbay.com — E-mail us at email@melbay.com

Contents

Foreword

The dream of Andres Segovia was to take the guitar out of the hands of the Spanish folklore guitarists, who performed mostly in taverns, and place it on the concert stage. He decided that in order to have the guitar receive the respect that he felt it deserved, it would need to be taught in the colleges, universities, and conservatories. Because of his intense concert career and his mature years, for his dream to be fulfilled he had to train teachers, who he called his disciples. Segovia accomplished his dream. Today the guitar has respect and credibility because of his vision and work. Bravo to the maestro!

While my performing career began in Miami nightclubs, much like the Spanish folklore guitarists, I went on to study with Segovia, who personally awarded me a scholarship that he paid for. I have performed on the concert stage with symphonic orchestras, and I am now a college professor. I have come to understand the significance of his dream.

Ironically, my dream is the complete opposite to that of Segovia. I believe that for the acoustic classical style to flourish, it must be put back into the hands of the people. My vision includes all guitarists, regardless of style or background, becoming familiar with the classical guitar technique and repertoire. To see my dream fulfilled, I have had to make learning fun and simple, without sacrificing the integrity of the information. By the mid 1980s my vision came to life in the form of a book entitled *A Rock Player's Guide to Classical Guitar*. It was the first classical guitar book that included the notation/tablature/tape format. I chose the rock market, because at that time they were the only guitarists who were genuinely interested and eager to learn "classical" from me. This, of course, didn't surprise me, since I too began as a rock guitarist. It was obvious that when classical guitar was accessible to all guitarists, more people would hear and enjoy the beauty of the pure guitar style. Since my first publication, thousands of new classical guitarists have surfaced.

All of my books come in notation/tablature/recording format. The recordings prove that all of my arrangements have been tested and do sound guitaristic. All of the great late composers were fine musicians, as well as composers. They could play the music they composed. You can also play the great classics! With the tablature and the recording, great music is closer to your fingertips than you might imagine.

Ben Bolt

About the Author

Ben Bolt is credited with being the first classical guitarist to introduce thousands of new people to the classical style of guitar through his videos and books, which use a revolutionary format of learning. In the past, guitar students needed to learn to read music at the same time they were learning to play the guitar, which was complicated. Since the publication of Bolt's book/recording packages, beginners are able to play immediately. The tablature, using lines and numbers to show where the notes are, and the recording, which is rhythmically self-explanatory, empowers all students to play. Bolt's work has been mimicked throughout the publishing world. Because of his vision of making classical guitar accessible to all kinds of musicians, the classic guitar is being experienced by the masses.

Andres Segovia, the father of classical guitar, said, "Ben Bolt is an excellent guitarist with fine tone." Segovia personally paid for a scholarship so that Bolt could continue his studies at the Musica en Compostela, which Segovia founded. During the Spanish Civil War Segovia had been in exile in Montevideo, Uruguay. He was not concertizing in Europe, due to World War II. Because of extra time, he took on one of his most talented students, Abel Carlevaro. Carlevaro took lessons every other day for over ten years in Uruguay. Because of this historic fact, Bolt sought out Carlevaro in order to attain more information about Segovia. In Paris Bolt studied with Maestro Carlevaro, who wanted to continue teaching Bolt in Brazil at the International Guitar Conservatory. There, under full scholarship Bolt was introduced to more Segovia information and, equally important, the Carlevaro school of technique. During the next several years he went on to Montevideo, Carlevaro's home town, and completed his music studies under the direction of Maestro Carlevaro and Guido Santorsola, the distinguished Italian composer and conductor.

Several Ben Bolt books have appeared on the best seller list. His video, *Anyone Can Play the Classic Guitar*, has become a reference for college students as the authority on basic fundamentals concerning classical technique. He also appears in Mel Bay's video of the *Modern Guitar Method Grade One*, a huge commercial success, selling millions of copies.

Bolt divides his time between publishing, performing with orchestras, and teaching at the college level. He believes anyone can play the guitar well, provided they have these three ingredients: a good instrument, a knowledgeable teacher, and music that holds the student's interest.

Bolt's work is distributed internationally and has been featured at the yearly NAMM show (National Association of Music Merchants) in California, as well as the International NAMM show in Germany. His influences include Mel Bay, the Beatles, and Segovia.

Other Titles

by Ben Bolt

Music Theory for the Rock Guitarist by Ben Bolt. (94525BCD) Written in notation and tablature, this fine text presents basic information on building and playing blues scales, octaves, pentatonic scales, double stops, passing notes, modes, diatonic and chromatic scales, and chords and arpeggios. The rock guitarist is shown the principles of chord and scale formation, as well as how to use various aspects of theory and harmony correctly in performance. Book/CD set.

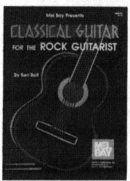

Classical Guitar for the Rock Guitarist by Ben Bolt. (94700BCD) Today's rock musicians are stretching the boundaries of their music by learning from the masters of various styles and disciplines. This book was carefully written by guitarist Ben Bolt, who is well acquainted with the styles and disciplines of both rock and classic guitar. It presents the essentials of classical guitar performance, musicianship, and phrasing in an easy-to-understand manner, and provides a wealth of beautiful and fun-to-play arrangements. All classic solos presented in this fine text are in notation and tablature. Selections include "Canon" by Pachelbel, "Anitra's Dance" by Grieg, "Pavane for a Dead Infant Princess" by Ravel, "Gymnopedie" by Satie, "Rondo Alla Turca" by Mozart, and many, many more! Book/CD set, video.

Note Reading for the Rock Guitarist by Ben Bolt. (94813BCD) Note reading is the key that can unlock the vast and exciting world of music. This unique and innovative system approaches it horizontally! Thus, instead of the usual manner of learning the natural notes in the first position, starting with the first string and going to the sixth, this method teaches all the natural notes on each string from left to right. In the author's words, "If you have tried to read music before and found yourself bored and frustrated, this book will give you hope." In notation and tablature. Book/CD set.

Anyone Can Play Classic Guitar Video taught by Ben Bolt. (95082VX) In this video, you will learn from one of America's foremost classic guitar teachers. Ben Bolt demonstrates his principles for judging distance, point of reference, right- and left-hand positions, and the correct sitting posture. An easy-to-understand and technically correct introduction to classic guitar performance. 45-minute video.

Favorite Classics for Acoustic Guitar by Ben Bolt. (95102BCD) Classic guitar virtuoso Ben Bolt has presented 15 all-time favorite classic guitar solos in notation and tablature. The solos cover many centuries of guitar and lute compositions and provide beautiful solo settings for classic or fingerstyle/steel-string guitarists. Book/CD set, video.

Mozart for Acoustic Guitar by Ben Bolt. (95526BCD) Because Mozart was a profoundly versatile composer, his music suits the guitar as well as it does a chamber orchestra. Playing this music on the guitar will impress your audience and provide a glimpse of Mozart's genius. Text is written in English, Spanish, French, and Japanese. In standard notation and tablature. Book/CD set.

Francisco Tárrega

Born on November 21, 1852, in Villareal, Spain, Francisco Tárrega was one of the most influential guitarists and composers of all time. While still a boy, he decided to become a guitarist after hearing popular guitarist Manuel Gonzalez play. He began his guitar studies with Gonzalez around the age of eleven, and later took lessons with Felix Ponza.

As a child he was pushed into a polluted stream by a ruthless nursemaid. He nearly drowned and his eyesight was seriously impaired, resulting in an incurable and painful eye disease known as ophthalmia. In later years he was reluctant to give public concerts and was more content to play for small groups of friends and pupils. This was directly related to the trauma of the childhood experience.

He completed his formal music studies in harmony, solfeo, piano, and composition, at the Madrid Conservatory of Music. In 1875 he was awarded the first prize for harmony and composition at age 23. In March of 1880 when he was 29 years old, he went to France, where his concerts in Paris were enthusiastically received. He later toured many parts of Europe with similar success. Tárrega is responsible for bringing the classic guitar to new heights with his original compositions and transcriptions for guitar. Because of his profound understanding of the instrument, including his romantic style and concept of fingering, virtually every classic guitarist has been influenced by this great artist. He died on December 15, 1909 in Barcelona.

In 1916 a monument was erected in his memory in Villareal. The plaque there bears the following inscription:

> "In this house was born on November 21, 1852, to the
> honor and glory of Villareal, the eminent guitarist
> Francisco Tárrega."

Throughout Spain streets have been named after him as a daily reminder and lasting tribute to this great man whose genius was only equaled by his warmth and modesty.

Ben Bolt

Romantic Guitar Masters
The Historic Lineage Across Two Centuries

Francisco Tárrega 1852–1909
Originator of Romantic Guitar Style

Miguel Llobet 1878–1938
Student of Francisco Tárrega
Maestro to Segovia

Andres Segovia 1893–1987
20th Century Father of Classical Guitar

Tablature

(Tab)

Tablature is an ancient way to write music. It is still used today because it is so easy to learn.

Tab is written on six lines. These six lines represent the six strings of the guitar. See examples.

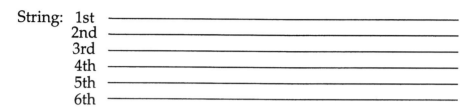

Numbers represent the spaces or frets to be played. This example means to play 1st, 3rd, and 5th frets in order of left to right, like reading words:

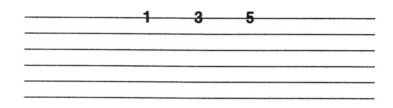

If the numbers are written in a vertical line, it means to play these numbers *simultaneously*.

E Chord

Music

Pitch

Music is written on five lines. These lines are called the **staff**. The notes can be written on the lines or in the spaces between the lines.

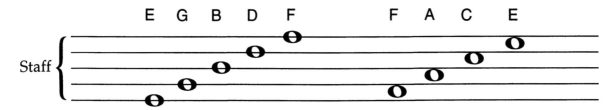

Notes above or below the staff require additional lines as a continuation of the staff. These lines are called **ledger lines**.

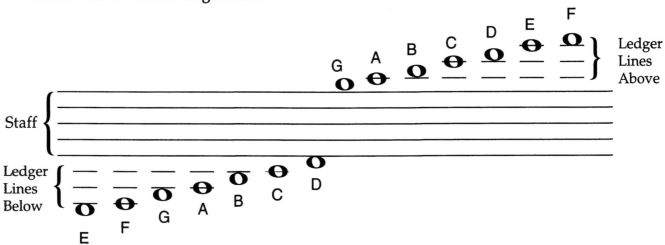

The musical alphabet uses the first seven letters of the language alphabet: A, B, C, D, E, F, G. After G, the next letter is A again. From any letter to the same letter is called an octave. There are eight letters in an octave.

One Octave: C D E F G A B C

At the beginning of every staff, you will notice a sign called the **clef sign**. In guitar music, we use the G or treble clef sign.

Sharps, Flats, and Naturals

Sharps, flats, and naturals raise or lower a note by 1 fret. A 1-fret distance on the guitar is called a **half step** in music (or **half tone**). Each sharp, flat, and natural has a sign that is placed before the note.

Sharp	♯	raises the note by 1 fret.
Flat	♭	lowers the note by 1 fret.
Natural	♮	restores the note to its regular pitch after it was raised or lowered.

The way a note is written determines the length of the note's duration

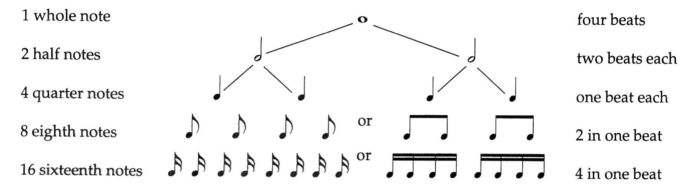

1 whole note		four beats
2 half notes		two beats each
4 quarter notes		one beat each
8 eighth notes	or	2 in one beat
16 sixteenth notes	or	4 in one beat

Rests

For every note value there is a corresponding rest having the same time value.

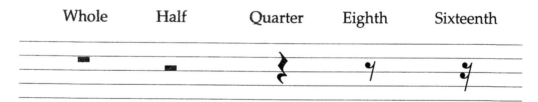

Whole   Half   Quarter   Eighth   Sixteenth

Music is arithmetically divided into **measures** by vertical bars in the staff. The number of beats in each measure is determined by the time signature placed after the clef.

$$\frac{2}{4} \quad \frac{3}{4} \quad \frac{4}{4} \quad \frac{3}{8} \quad \frac{6}{8} \quad \text{etc.}$$

The top number tells how many beats in a measure, while the bottom number tells what kind of note receives one beat.

$\begin{array}{l}\mathbf{3} \\ \mathbf{4}\end{array}$ $\begin{array}{l}= \\ =\end{array}$ three beats to the measure
1 quarter note per beat
or the equivalent:
2 eighth notes per beat
or 4 sixteenth notes per beat, etc.

The most common time signature is $\begin{array}{l}\mathbf{4} \\ \mathbf{4}\end{array}$. It is also marked **C**.

Key Signature

When the tonality requires that certain notes are to be sharp or flat throughout a composition, the sharps or flats are grouped together at the beginning of each staff, forming the key signature. This affects every note of the same name throughout the musical piece.

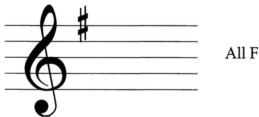   All F notes are to be played F sharp.

The Dot

A dot placed to the right of a note lengthens it by one half:

$$\downarrow \cdot = \, \flat \flat \flat$$

These dots can also be placed to the right of rests:

$$\xi \cdot = \, \gamma \, \gamma \, \gamma$$

The Double Sharp

A double sharp placed before a note raises it by 2 frets, or a whole tone. G double sharp will sound like A. The sign looks like this:

𝄪

12

The Double Flat

The double flat lowers a note 2 frets, or a whole tone. E double flat will sound like D.
The sign uses two flats before a note:

Repeats

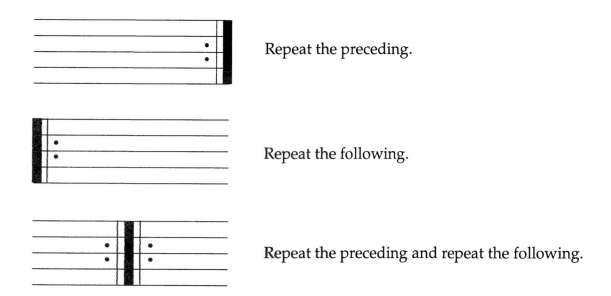

Repeat the preceding.

Repeat the following.

Repeat the preceding and repeat the following.

The Right Hand

Fingering

English	Symbol	Spanish
Thumb	= *p* =	Pulgar
Index	= *i* =	Indice
Middle	= *m* =	Medio
Ring	= *a* =	Anular

Position

The best way to learn a good right-hand position is to place *i, m,* and *a* on the third string.
Place your thumb on the third string as well, keeping the thumb to the left of the index finger.
(See sketch.)

The Right Hand

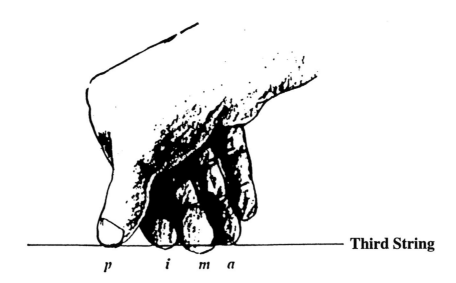

p   i   m   a   **Third String**

Strokes

The rest stroke using the thumb: Place *a* on the first string, *m* on the second string, and *i* on the third string. Play the sixth string slowly. As you glide over the string, follow through until you reach the fifth string. You should end up resting on the string number 5. Practice on all bass strings (6, 5, and 4).

The rest stroke using the fingers: Place the thumb (*p*) on the sixth string. Play the third string slowly with your index (*i*) finger. As your finger glides slowly over the string, follow through until you rest on string number 4. Practice using your middle finger (*m*) on the second string and your ring finger (*a*) on the first string. Also, practice alternating *im, ia,* and *ma* on the treble strings (1, 2, and 3). I use *i* and *a* because they are similar in length on my hand. You should collapse the joint closest to the tip of the finger during the follow-through.

Free stroke: In using free stroke, the finger does not rest. The joint closest to the tip of the finger does not collapse. You must be careful not to get under the string and pull up with the finger. As an experiment, you can try pulling the string straight up and releasing it. This will cause a slap against the fingerboard and should be avoided. However, rock bass players use this technique as an effect that sounds good!

Regardless of which stroke is used, the flesh and fingernail should touch the string at the same time when you're preparing to play. This technique produces the best tone.

The Left Hand

Fingering

Index	=	1
Middle	=	2
Ring	=	3
Little Finger	=	4

Position

Because music changes pitch and direction, the left hand also needs to follow that motion. This makes explaining the left-hand position difficult, because it depends on your technical needs at that time. However, there are some practical and general concepts to keep in mind.

First, the fingernails of the left hand should be short enough so that they do not touch the fingerboard of the guitar. Second, the thumb should be placed generally in the middle of the back of the neck between the index and middle fingers. (See sketch.)

Third, the fingers should always be placed directly behind the frets. This gives the best tone and helps to teach your arm and finger exactly where each note is. Correct muscular memory begins here. Last, when playing scale passages, the knuckles should be parallel to the fingerboard.

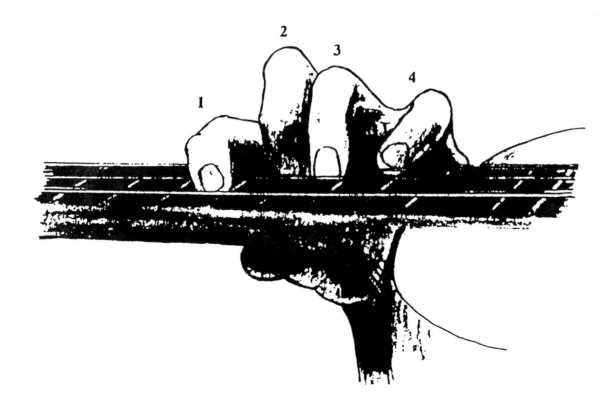

Francisco Tárrega

Introducción

El sueño de Andres Segovia era tomar la guitarra de las manos de los guitarristas folklóricos españoles, quienes tocaban principalmente en bares, y elevarla a la categoría de concierto. Él decidio que sería necesario enseñar la guitarra en universidades y conservatorios para que ésta recibiera el respeto que merecía. Debido a su intensa carrera como concertista y a su avanzada edad, tuvo que entrenar maestros, a los cuales llamo discípulos, para completar su sueño. Segovia logró su ideal. En nuestros días, la guitarra es vista con respeto y credibilidad debido a su visión y trabajo. ¡Bravo por el maestro!

Aunque mi carrera comenzó en clubes nocturnos de Miami, como la de los guitarristas del folklore español, estudié con Segovia quien personalmente sufragó mis estudios. He compartido el escenario con orquestas sinfónicas y actualmente soy profesor a nivel universitario. Ahora he llegado a entender el significado de su sueño.

Irónicamente, mi sueño es completamente opuesto al de Segovia. Pienso que para que el estilo de la guitarra acústica florezca, es necesario devolverla a las manos del pueblo. Mi sueño incluye guitarristas de todos los estilos empezando a familiarizarse con la técnica y repertorio de la guitarra clásica. Para hacer mi sueño realidad, he tenido que hacer el aprendizaje simple y entretenido, pero nunca sacrificando la integridad del contenido. A mediados de los 80s, mi sueño tomó vida en la forma del libro titulado "Guitarra clásica para el guitarrista rock". Aquel fue el primer libro de guitarra clásica que incluyó notación/tablatura y cinta. Escogí el mercado del rock porque en aquel tiempo ellos eran los únicos interesados en aprender guitarra clásica con mi ayuda. Esto no me sorprendió en lo absoluto porque yo empecé como guitarrista de rock también. Era obvio que cuando la guitarra clásica fuera accesible a todos los guitarristas, más gente escucharía y disfrutaría la belleza del estilo puro. Desde mi primera publicación, miles de nuevos guitarristas del estilo "clásico" han surgido.

Todos mis libros están escritos en notación/tablatura y cinta. Esta es la forma utilizada por las grandes casas editoriales. Las cintas demuestran que todas mis composiciones han sido probadas y son producidas por una guitarra.

Ben Bolt
Traducción de Haydee O. Casado

El autor

Ben Bolt ha sido reconocido como el primer guitarrista en introducir miles de personas al estilo de guitarra "clásica" a través de sus videos y libros, los cuales usan una manera de aprendizaje revolucionaria. En el pasado, estudiantes de guitarra necesitaban aprender a leer música al mismo tiempo que aprendían a tocar la guitarra. Esto era realmente complicado. Desde la publicación de los paquetes libro/cassette de Bolt, estudiantes que están comenzando pueden empezar a tocar de inmediato. La tablatura, que usa líneas y números para mostrar donde estan las notas, y el cassette, que se explica por si mismo rítmicamente, permite a todos los estudiantes tocar. El trabajo de Bolt ha sido imitado por casas editoras del medio. La guitarra clásica ha sido mostrada a las masas gracias a su visión de hacerla accesible a todo tipo de músicos.

Andrés Segovia, el padre de la guitarra clásica, dijo: "Ben Bolt es un guitarrista excelente con un tono fino". Segovia pagó personalmente para que Bolt continuara sus estudios en Música en Compostela, fundada por Segovia. Durante la guerra civil de España, Segovia fue exiliado en Montevideo, Uruguay. Durante este tiempo, no se estaba presentando en Europa debido a la segunda guerra mundial. Él llevo consigo a uno de sus estudiantes más talentosos, Abel Carlevaro. Carlevaro tomó lecciones tres o cuatro días a la semana por diez años en Uruguay. Debido a este dato histórico, Bolt buscó a Carlevaro para obtener más infamación acerca de Segovia. En París, Bolt estudio con el Maestro Carlevaro quien después quiso continuar enseñándole en el Conservatorio Internacional de Guitarra en Brasil. Allí, con una beca, Bolt fue introducido con más infamación sobre Segovia, pero también con la escuela técnica de Carlevaro. Durante los años siguientes él fue a Montevideo, el pueblo natal de Carlearo, y completó sus estudios bajo la dirección del Maestro Carlevaro y Guido Santorsola, el distinguido compositor y director italiano.

Muchos de los libros de Bolt han aparecido en la lista de los mejores vendidos. Su video "Cualquiera Puede Tocar La Guitarra Clásica" se ha convertido en referencia para estudiantes universitarios como la autoridad en principios básicos sobre técnica "clásica" Además él aparece en el video "Método Moderno para la Guitarra, Libro 1" de Mel Bay. El video ha sido un gran éxito comercial y ha vendido millones de copias.

Bolt pasa su tiempo publicando, presentándose con orquestas y enseñando a nivel universitario. Él esta convencido que cualquiera puede tocar bien la guitarra, siempre y cuando los siguientes ingredientes estén presentes: un buen instrumento, un maestro preparado y música que estimule el interés del estudiante.

El trabajo de Bolt es distribuido internacionalmente y ha sido presentado anualmente en el show de la NAMM (Asociación Nacional de Comerciantes de Música) en California, así como también en el show internacional en Alemania.

Otros Títulos

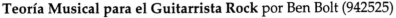

por Ben Bolt (en inglés)

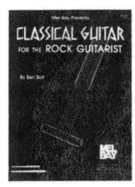

Teoría Musical para el Guitarrista Rock por Ben Bolt (942525)
Escrito en notación y tablatura, este libro presenta información básica sobre cómo construir y tocar escalas de blues, octavas, escalas pentatónicas, notas de paso, modos, escalas diatónicas y cromáticas, acordes y arpegios. El guitarrista rock es presentado con los principios de la formación de acordes y escalas, además de como usar correctamente los variados aspectos de la teoría y armonía en presentaciones.

Guitarra Clásica para el Guitarrista Rock por Ben Bolt. (94700)
Hoy día, los músicos rock estan extendiendo las barreras de su música aprendiendo de los maestros de varios estilos y disciplinas. Este libro fue escrito cuidadosamente por el guitarrista Ben Bolt, quien esta bien relacionado con los estilos y disciplinas tanto de la guitarra rock como de la clásica. El libro presenta los principios esenciales sobre cómo tocar la guitarra clásica, usar musicalidad y fraseo en una manera fácil de entender. Además provee un tesoro de hermosas y amenas piezas para tocar. Todos los solos clásicos presentados es este valioso libro están en notación y tablatura. Están incluidos "Canon" de Pachelbel, "Danza de Anitra" de Grieg, "Pavana para una infanta difunta" de Ravel, "Gymnopedie" de Satie, "Rondo Alla Turca" de Mozart, y muchos más!

Lectura Musical para el Guitarrista Rock por Ben Bolt. (94813)
La lectura de notas es la llave que puede abrir el vasto y excitante mundo de la música. ¡Este sistema único e innovador entra a este mundo horizontalmente! De forma que en vez de usar la manera común de aprender las notas naturales en la primera posición, este método enseña todas las notas naturales en cada cuerda de izquierda a derecha, empezando con la primera cuerda y avanzando hasta la sexta. En las palabras del autor, "Si has tratado de leer música antes y te has encontrado aburrido y frustrado, este libro te dará esperanza." En notación y tablatura.

Cualquiera Puede Tocar Guitarra Clásica, video por Ben Bolt. (95082VX)
En este video, aprenderás de uno de los mejores guitarristas "clásicos" de Norteamérica. Ben Bolt muestra sus principios para juzgar distancia, punto de referencia, posiciones de la mano izquierda y derecha, y la forma correcta de sentarse. Una introducción a la guitarra clásica fácil de entender y técnicamente correcta.

Clásicos Favoritos para Guitarra Acústica por Ben Bolt (95102)
El virtuoso de la Guitarra Clásica Ben Bolt presenta 15 favoritos de todos los tiempos en notación y tablatura. Los solos cubren muchos siglos de composiciones para guitarra y laúd y proveen el escenario perfecto para guitarristas del estilo clásico o guitarristas que usan cuerdas de metal.

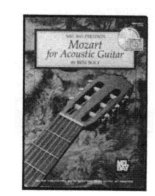

Tablatura

La Tablatura es una manera antigua de escribir música. Todavía es usada en nuestros días porque es muy fácil de aprender.

La Tablatura se escribe en seis líneas. Estas seis líneas representan las seis cuerdas de la guitarra. Ver ejemplo.

Cuerdas: 1a
          2a
          3a
          4a
          5a
          6a

Los números representan los espacios o trastes que deben ser tocados. Este ejemplo significa que se debe tocar el 1er, 3er y 5to traste en orden de izquierda a derecha, como si se estuviera leyendo:

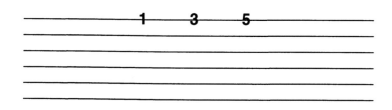

Si los números están escritos en una línea vertical significa que se deben tocar estos números simultáneamente.

Acorde Mi

Música

Tono o altura

La música se escribe sobre cinco líneas. Estas cinco líneas son llamadas **pentagrama**. Las notas pueden ser escritas sobre las líneas o en los espacios entre las líneas.

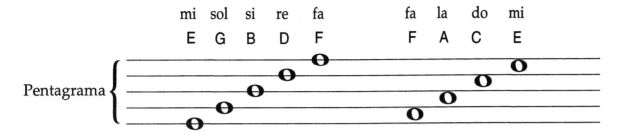

Las notas escritas encima o debajo del pentagrama requieren líneas extras como continuación del mismo. Estas líneas son llamadas **líneas adicionales.**

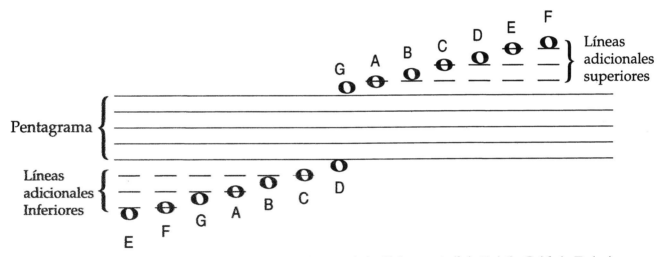

El alfabeto musical usa las siete primera letras del alfabeto: A (la), B (si), C (do), D (re), E (mi), F (fa), G (sol). Después de G, viene A otra vez. Desde una letra hasta la misma letra se llama una **octava.** Hay ocho letras en una octava.

Una octava: C   D   E   F   G   A   B   C

Al comienzo de cada pentagrama notarás un signo llamado la **clave**. En la musica para guitarra usamos la clave de sol.

Clave de sol

Los sostenidos, bemoles y becuadros

Suben o bajan una nota un traste. La distancia de un traste en la guitarra es llamada **semitono** (o medio tono). Cada alteración tiene un signo antes de la nota.

Sostenido ♯ sube la nota un traste.

Bemol ♭ baja la nota un traste.

Becuadro ♮ regresa la nota a su tono natural después de haberse subido o bajado.

La figura de una nota determina la duración de la misma:

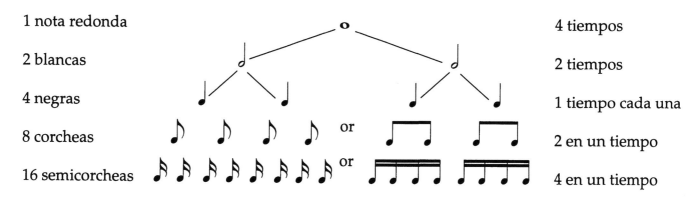

1 nota redonda		4 tiempos
2 blancas		2 tiempos
4 negras		1 tiempo cada una
8 corcheas		2 en un tiempo
16 semicorcheas		4 en un tiempo

Silencios

Para cada nota hay un silencio sorrespondiente, con el mismo valor.

Redonda   Blanca   Negra   Corchea   Semicorchea

La música esta aritméticamente dividida en medidas llamadas **compases** por barras verticales en el pentagrama. El numero de tiempos en cada medida esta determinado por el compás colocado después de la clave.

$$\frac{2}{4} \quad \frac{3}{4} \quad \frac{4}{4} \quad \frac{3}{8} \quad \frac{6}{8}$$ etc.

El número superior indica el número de tiempos, mientras que el número inferior indica la clase de nota que recibe un tiempo.

3 = tres tiempos en la medida.
4 = una negra por tiempo o el equivalente:
dos corcheas por tiempo o cuatro
semicorcheas por tiempo, etc.

El signo de tiempo más común es $\frac{4}{4}$. También se marca **C** (compasillo).

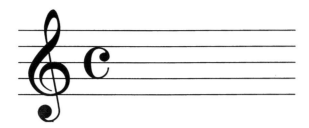

Armadura de clave

Cuando la tonalidad requiere que ciertas notas sean sostenidos o bemoles a lo largo de una composición, los bemoles o sostenidos son agrupados al principio de cada pentagrama, formando la armadura de clave. Esta afecta cada nota del mismo nombre a lo largo de la pieza musical.

   Todas las notas F (fa) deben ser sostenidas.

El puntillo

Un punto colocado a la derecha de una nota la alarga la mitad de su valor:

$$\text{♩.} = \text{♪♪♪}$$

Estos puntos pueden ser colocados tambien a la derecha de los silencios:

El doble sostenido

Un doble sostenido colocado delante de una nota la sube dos trastes, o un tono completo. Un G doble sostenido suena como A. El signo es el siguiente:

𝄪

El doble bemol

El doble bemol baja la nota dos trastes, o un tono completo. La nota E (mi) doble bemol suena como D (re). Este signo utiliza dos bemoles delante de una nota:

Repeticiones

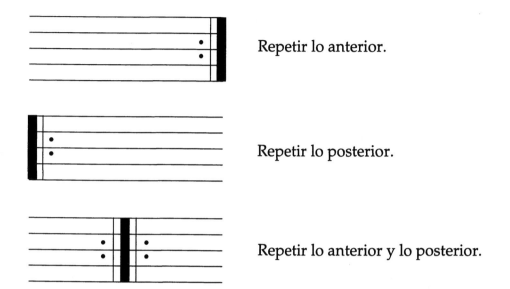

Repetir lo anterior.

Repetir lo posterior.

Repetir lo anterior y lo posterior.

La mano derecha

Digitación

Símbolo		Español
p	=	Pulgar
i	=	Indice
m	=	Medio
a	=	Anular

Posición

La mejor forma de aprender la posición correcta de la mano derecha es poniendo *i, m, y a* en la tercera cuerda. Ponga el pulgar en la tercera cuerda también, colocándolo a la izquierda del dedo índice. (Ver diagrama).

Mano derecha

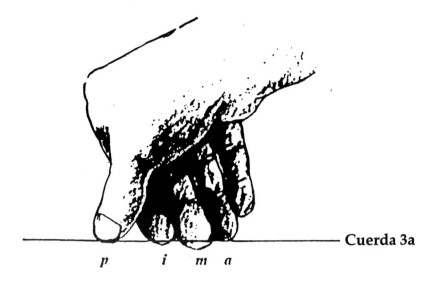

Cuerda 3a

p   i   m   a

Pulsaciones

Apoyando usando el pulgar: Pon el dedo *a* en la primera cuerda, *m* en la segunda, *i* en la tercera. Toca la sexta cuerda lentamente. Al tocarla, continúa hasta llegar a la quinta. Debes terminar descansando el dedo en la quinta cuerda. Practica con todos los bajos (6ta., 5ta., y 4ta. cuerda).

Apoyando usando los dedos: Colocar el pulgar *(p)* sobre la sexta cuerda. Tocar la tercera cuerda lentamente con el dedo índice *(i)*. Mientras tu dedo se desliza lentamente sobre la cuerda, continúa hasta descansar sobre la cuerda número cuatro. Practicar lo mismo usando dedo medio *(m)* sobre la segunda cuerda y el anular *(a)* sobre la primera. Además, practicar alternando *im, ia,* y *ma* sobre las cuerdas (1ra., 2da., y 3ra.). Yo uso *i* y *a* porque son similares en longitud en mi mano. Debes hundir la articulación más cercana a la punta del dedo al final del movimiento .

Tirando: Al usar tirando, los dedos no descansan en la cuerda anterior. La articulación más cercana a la punta del dedo no se hunde. Debes tener cuidado de no halar la cuerda con el dedo. A manera de experimento, puedes tratar de halar la cuerda hacia arriba desde abajo y soltarla. La cuerda chocará contra los trastes y ésto debe ser evitado. Bajistas rock usan esta técnica como efecto y suena bien.

Sin embargo cualquiera que sea el golpe usado, uña y carne deben tocar la cuerda al mismo tiempo cuando te dispongas a tocar. Esta técnica produce el mejor sonido.

La mano izquierda

Digitación

1	=	índice
2	=	medio
3	=	anular
4	=	pequeño o meñique

Posición

Como la música fluctúa en altura y dirección, la mano izquierda necesita seguir ese proceder. Esto hace difícil explicar la posición de la mano izquierda, porque depende de la necesidad técnica del pasaje. Sin embargo, hay algunos conceptos prácticos y generales a considerar.

Primero: las uñas de la mano izquierda deberán ser suficientemente cortas para no tocar el diapasón de la guitarra.

Segundo: El pulgar debe colocarse generalmente detrás del cuello o diapasón entre los dedos índice y medio. (observar dibujo).

Tercero: los dedos deberán colocarse directamente detrás de los trastes. Esto produce el mejor sonido y ayuda al brazo y dedos encontrar el lugar de cada nota. La correcta memoria muscular comienza aquí. Por último, al tocar pasajes de escalas, los nudillos deberán estar paralelos al diapasón.

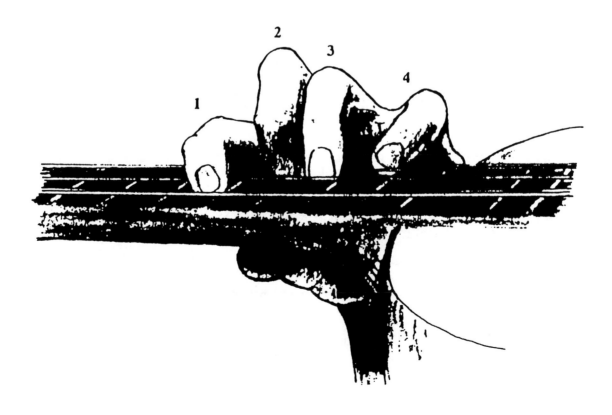

Miguel Llobet, giving pointers to friends and pupils.
Young Segovia is sitting in front, wearing his glasses.

Introduction

Le rêve du Maître André Segovia était de retirer la guitare des mains des guitaristes folkloriques espagnols, qui ne la jouaient plus la plupart que dans les tavernes, et de l'introduire dans les salles de concert. Il se rendit compte que la guitare devrait être enseignée dans les collèges, les universités et les conservatoires afin de recevoir le respect qu'elle méritait. Afin d'atteindre ce but, ayant eu une intensive carrière comme concertiste et, de par sa maturité, il dut enseigner d'autres professeurs de guitare qu'il appela ses disciples. Segovia réalisa son rêve. Aujourd'hui, par sa vision et son travail la guitare a gagné le respect et la credibilité. Bravo au maître!

Alors que ma carrière de musicien avait débuté dans les clubs (comme les guitaristes folkloristes espagnols) à Miami, je m'en allai continuer mes études avec Segovia qui m'attribua une bourse qu'il paya lui-même. J'ai joué dans les salles de concerts avec des orchestres symphoniques et maintenant j'enseigne la guitare dans les collèges. J'ai appris à reconnaître l'importance du rêve de Segovia

L'ironie est que mon rêve est totalement à l'opposé de celui de Segovia. Je pense qu'afin que la guitare acoustique s'épanouisse, elle doit retourner dans les mains du peuple. Tous les guitaristes sont compris dans ma vision, quelque soit leur style et expérience, devenant familier avec la technique et le répertoire de la guitare classique. Afin de réaliser mon rêve, j'ai dû faire de l'instruction une expérience simple et amusante, sans pour autant sacrifier l'integrité des informations . Dans les années 80, ma vision prit la forme d'un livre intitulé "la guitare classique pour le guitariste de rock." C'était le premier de ce genre comprenant la musique, les tablatures et les cassettes. J'avais choisi de m'adresser au milieu des guitaristes de rock, parce qu'à cette période ils étaient les seuls à exprimer un véritable intérêt ainsi que le désir d'apprendre le classique par mon intermédiaire. Je n'étais pas trop surpris ayant moi même commencé par la guitare de rock. Il était évident qu'une fois que la guitare classique deviendrait accessible a tous les guitaristes, plus de gens écouteraient et apprecieraient la beauté de ce style pur de la guitare. Des milliers de nouveaux guitaristes classiques ont surgi depuis ma première publication.

Tous mes livres sont publiés dans le même format avec la musique, les tablatures et les cassettes, qui depuis ont été copiés par les plus grands éditeurs de musique. Les cassettes démontrent que tous mes arrangements ont été mis à l'épreuve et que leurs musicalités conviennent parfaitement à la guitare.

Ben Bolt
Translation by Frederic Leyd

A propos de l'auteur

Ben Bolt a été crédité pour être le premier guitariste classique à introduire les milliers de personnes au style de la guitare classique à travers ses videos et ses livres, utilisant un format d'approche révolutionnaire. Dans le passé les étudiants devaient apprendre à lire la musique et à jouer la guitare en même temps, ce qui était compliqué. Depuis la publication des livres et des cassettes de Bolt, les débutants sont capables de jouer immédiatement. Les tablatures utilisant des lignes et des numéros pour montrer où sont les notes, et les cassettes exprimant le rythme, encouragent les étudiants à jouer. Le travail de Bolt a été copié à travers le monde de la publication musicale. A cause de son désir de rendre accessible la guitare à tous les styles de musiciens, la guitare classique est maintenant appreciée par les masses.

André Segovia, le père de la guitare classique avait dit: "Ben Bolt est un excellent guitariste avec un son raffiné". Segovia avait personnellement payé pour la bourse de Bolt afin qu'il puisse continuer ses études à la "Música en Compostela", que Segovia avait lui-même fondé. Pendant la guerre civile d'Espagne, Segovia était en éxil à Montevideo en Uruguay. Il ne faisait pas de concert en Europe à cause de la seconde guerre mondiale. Ayant du temps, il prit un de ses étudiants des plus talentueux, Abel Carlevaro. Carlevaro prit des leçons tous les deux jours pendant plus de dix ans en Uruguay. A cause de ce fait historique, Bolt rechercha Carlevaro pour obtenir plus d'information à propos de Segovia. A Paris Bolt étudia avec le maitre Carlevaro qui voulait continuer à l'enseigner au Brésil au Conservatoire International de la guitare. Là-bas, avec une bourse complète, Bolt reçut encore plus d'information à propos de Segovia, mais d'aussi grande importance, il fut introduit à l'école technique de Carlevaro. Pendant les quelques années suivantes il continua a Montevideo, la ville mère de Carlevaro, et compléta ses études de musique sous la direction du maître Carlevaro et du guide Santorsola, le compositeur et chef d'orchestre Italien distingué.

Plusieurs livres de Bolt ont paru sur la liste des "best seller". Sa cassette video "quiconque peut jouer de la guitare classique" est devenue une référence pour les étudiants de collèges offrant les éléments de bases de la technique classique. Il fit aussi une apparition dans le video de Mel Bay " methode de 1a guitare, livre 1", qui fut un gros succès commercial, vendu à des millions d'exemplaires. Bolt divise son temps entre ses publications, ses concerts avec les orchestres et ses cours au collège. Il croit que tout le monde peut bien jouer de la guitare si on est pourvu de ces trois ingrédients: un bon instrument, un enseignant érudit et de la musique intéressante pour l'étudiant.

Le travail de Bolt est distribué internationalement et présenté à la convention annuelle de la NAMM (National Association of Music Merchants), en Californie et en Allemagne.

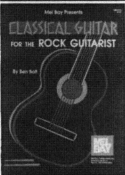

Les autres titres par Ben Bolt

Théorie de la musique pour le guitariste de rock par Ben Bolt. (94525) Utilisant la musique et les tablatures, cet excellent texte vous donne les informations de base afin de construire et de jouer les gammes du blues, les octaves, les gammes du solo, deux notes simultanément, les modulations, les modes, les gammes diatoniques et chromatiques, les différents accords et les arpèges. Il est montré au guitariste de rock le principe de la formation des accords et des gammes, ainsi que les aspects variés de l'utilisation de la théorie et de l'harmonie en concert. Livre, cassette.

La guitare classique pour le guitarist de rock par Ben Bolt. (94700). Les musiciens de rock d'aujourd'hui agrandissent les limites de leur musique en apprenant des maîtres de tout autre style et de leurs disciplines. Ce livre a été écrit avec soin par le guitariste Ben Bolt, qui est familier avec les deux styles de la guitare, classique et rock. Ce livre présente l'essentiel de la guitare classique de concert ainsi qu'une description de ce qu'il est attendu du concertiste professionnel, et d'une façon simple explique la formation de la phrase musicale, donnant ainsi la richesse et la joie de jouer ces très beaux arrangements. Tous les solos classiques représentés dans cette édition sont écrits avec l'aide de la musique et des tablatures. La sélection comprend: "Les canons" de Pachelbel, "La danse d'Anitra" de Grieg, "Pavane pour une infante défunte" de Ravel, "Gymnopedie" de Satre, "Rondo a la Turca" de Mozart, et bien d'autres! Livre, cassette, video.

La lecture et le manche, pour le guitariste de rock par Ben Bolt.(94813). La lecture des notes est la clé pouvant ouvrir le monde vaste et excitant de la musique. Ce sistème unique et innovateur l'approche d'une manière horizontale! Ainsi, au lieu d'utiliser la méthode habituelle qui est d'aprendre les notes naturelles en première position, commençant sur la première corde et allant jusqu'à la sixième, cette méthode enseigne toutes les notes naturelles sur une corde à la fois allant de gauche à droite. Dans les propres termes de l'auteur: "Si vous avez essayé auparavant de lire la musique et vous êtes trouvé enuyé et frustré, ce livre vous donnera de l'espoir." Musique et tablature. Livre, cassette.

"Tout le monde peut jouer de la guitare classique", en video, enseigné par Ben Bolt. (9S082VX). Dans cette cassette video vous serez enseigné par un des plus grands professeurs americains, Ben Bolt vous présente son principe pour évaluer la distance, le point de référence, les positions des mains et la posture correcte. Une introduction à la guitare qui est à la fois facile à comprendre et techniquement correcte. Video de 45 minutes.

Les classiques favoris pour la guitare acoustique, par Ben Bolt. Catalogue N 9S102. Le virtuose de la guitare classique, Ben Bolt a présenté 15 solos des préférés de la guitare classique avec la musique et les tablatures. Ces solos couvrent plusieurs centaines de compositions pour la guitare et le luth, vous donnant de superbes arrangements solos pour la guitare classique, pouvant aussi être joués sur une guitare à cordes métalliques.Livre, cassette, video.

Chiffrage et tablature

L'utilisation des tablatures est une ancienne manière d'écrire la musique. Elle est encore employée aujourd'hui étant si facile à apprendre.

Les tablatures sont écrites sur six lignes. Les six lignes représentent les cordes de la guitare. Voir l'exemple:

Cordes: 1ère
        2ième
        3ième
        4ième
        5ième
        6ième

Les numéros correspondent aux cases à jouer.
Cet exemple indique qu'il faut jouer la 1ére, 3ième et 5ième case allant de gauche à droite, comme la lecture de mots.

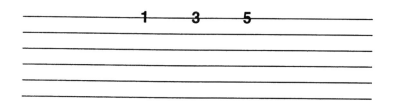

Si les numéros sont écrits verticalement, cela voudrait dire qu'il faut jouer ces numéros simultanément.

Accord de Mi (E)

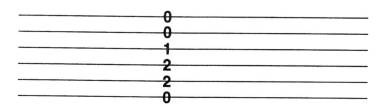

Solfège

Le ton

Le solfège est écrit sur cinq lignes. Ces lignes constituent la **portée**. Les notes peuvent être écrites sur et entre les lignes.

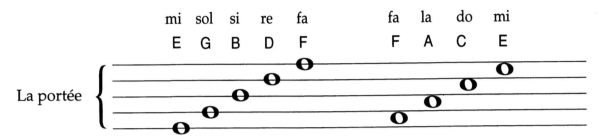

Les notes au-dessus et en dessous de la portée demande l'addition de lignes. Ces lignes sont appelées **Lignes supplémentaires.**

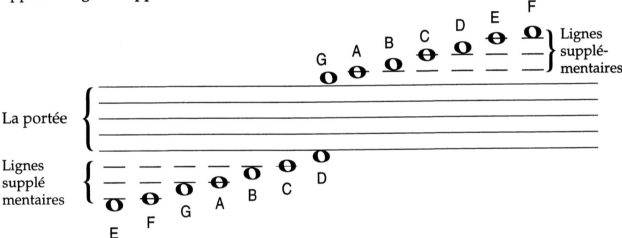

Dans le langage international de la musique, on emploie les sept premières lettres de l'alphabet: A, B, C, D, E, F, G. Après G, la prochaine lettre serait A de nouveau. D'une lettre à la même lettre constitue l'**octave**. Il y a huit lettres dans un octave.

Un octave: C D E F G A B C

Au début de chaque portée, vous noterez un signe appelé la clé. La musique écrite pour la guitare utilise la clé de sol.

La clé de sol

Le dièse, le bémol et le bécarre

Le dièse, le bémol et le bécarre élèvent ou abaissent une note par une barre. On appelle la distance d'une barre sur la guitare un demi-ton. Chaque dièse, bémol et bécarre est caracterisé par un signe placé devant la note.

Le dièse ♯ élève la note d'une barre.

Le bémol ♭ abaisse la note d'une barre.

Le bécarre ♮ retourne la note à son ton naturel après avoir été élevé ou abaissé.

La manière d'écrire une note détermine la durée pour laquelle elle sera jouée.

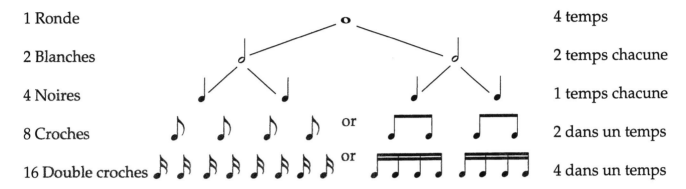

1 Ronde		4 temps
2 Blanches		2 temps chacune
4 Noires		1 temps chacune
8 Croches	or	2 dans un temps
16 Double croches	or	4 dans un temps

La pause

Chaque valeur de note a une pause correspondante de la même durée.

La pause   la demi-pause   le soupir   le demi-soupir   le quart de soupir

La musique est arithmétiquement divisée par des mesures utilisant des barres verticales sur la portée. Le nombre de temps dans chaque mesure est déterminé par le temps placé après la clé:

$$\frac{2}{4} \quad \frac{3}{4} \quad \frac{4}{4} \quad \frac{3}{8} \quad \frac{6}{8} \quad \text{etc.}$$

Le numéro du dessus détermine le nombre de temps par mesure, alors que celui du bas indique quelle valeur de note constitue un temps.

$\begin{array}{ll} 3 & = \text{trois temps par mesure.} \\ 4 & = \text{une noire par temps ou l'equivalent: 2} \\ & \text{croches par temps ou 4 double croches} \\ & \text{par temps, etc.} \end{array}$

Le temps le plus commun est $\frac{4}{4}$. Il est aussi écrit ainsi **C**.

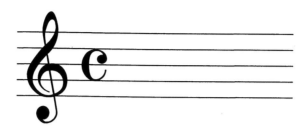

Le ton

Quand la tonalité demande que certaines notes soient dièses ou bémol au cours de la composition, les dièses et les bémols sont trouvés groupés au début de chaque portée, indicant la tonalité. Cela touche toutes les notes du même nom au cours de la pièce musicale.

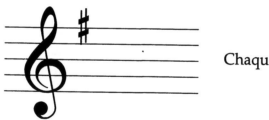   Chaque fa devra être joué fa dièse.

Le point

Un point placé a la droite d'une note étend sa valeur par la moitié:

$$\text{♩.} = \text{♪♪♪}$$

Un point peu être aussi placé à la droite d'un silence:

$$\text{𝄾.} = \text{⅞ ⅞ ⅞}$$

Le double dièse

Un double dièse placé devant une note l'élève de deux cases, ou d'un ton. Sol précèdé d'un double dièse sonnera comme un la Le symbole ressemble à ceci:

$$\text{𝄪}$$

Le double bémol

Le double bémol descent une note de 2 cases ou d'un ton complet Double bémol E se jouera comme un D. Le signe s'écrit utilisant deux bémols devant la note:
:

Les reprises

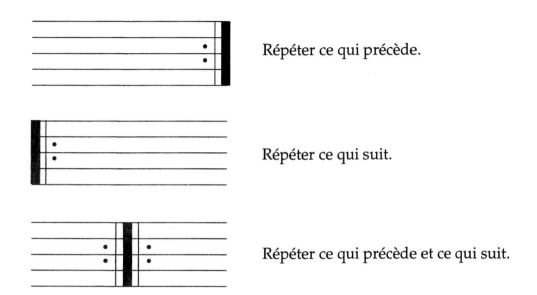

Répéter ce qui précède.

Répéter ce qui suit.

Répéter ce qui précède et ce qui suit.

La main droite

Le doigté

Français	Símbolo			Español
Français	= p	=		Pulgar
Index	= i	=		Indice
Majeur	= m	=		Medio
Majeur	= a	=		Anular

La position

La meilleure manière d'apprendre la bonne position pour la main droite, est de placer *i*, *m*, et *a* sur la troisième corde Mettez aussi votre pouce sur la troisième corde, le plaçant sur la gauche de votre index (Voir figure).

Pouce

Annulaire

La main droite

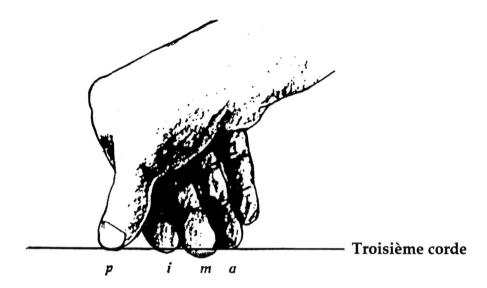

Troisième corde

p   i   m   a

L'attaque

Le butté utilisant le pouce: Placez a sur la première corde, m sur la deuxième corde, et i sur la troisième corde. Jouez la sixième corde doucement. Glisser sur la corde et continuez jusqu'a ce que vous atteigniez la cinquième corde Vous devriez finir reposant sur la cinquième corde. Répéter sur toutes les cordes basses (6, 5 et 4).

Le butté utilisant les doigts: Placez votre pouce *(p)* sur la sixième corde. Jouez la troisième corde avec l'index *(i)*. Glissez sur la corde et continuez jusqu'a ce que vous reposiez sur la corde numero 4. Répéter utilisant votre majeur *(m)* sur la deuxième corde et l'annulaire *(a)* sur la première corde. Répéter aussi alternant *im, ia* et *ma* sur les cordes aiguës (1,2 et 3) J'utilise i et a parce qu'ils sont de la même longueur sur ma main. Vous devriez relâcher la phalange la plus proche du bout du doigt suivant l'attaque.

L'arpège: Utiliser l'arpège veut dire que le doigt ne se pose pas suivant l'attaque. La phalange la plus proche du bout du doigt ne se relâche pas. Attention de ne pas aller sous la corde et de la tirer au loin du plan des cordes. Faites l'expérience de tirer sur la corde horizontalement et de la relâcher. Cela cause la corde de frapper le manche et ceci devrait être évité. Néanmoins les bassistes de rock utilisent cette technique pour créer un bon effet!

Quelque soit l'attaque utilisée, le pouce et l'ongle devraient toucher la corde en même temps lorsque vous vous préparez a jouer. Cette technique produit le meilleur son.

La main gauche

Le doigté

Index	= 1
Majeur	= 2
Annulaire	= 3
Auriculaire	= 4

La position

Parce que la musique change de ton et de direction, la main gauche a aussi besoin de suivre ce mouvement Cela rend la position de la main gauche difficile a expliquer, parce qu'elle dépend de votre besoin technique du moment. Néanmoins il y a quelques concepts généraux pratiques à se souvenir

Premièrement, les ongles de la main gauche doivent être courts afin de ne pas toucher les touches Deuxièmement, en général le pouce devrait être placé au milieu du dos du manche entre l'index et le majeur. (Voir figure).

Troisièmement, les doigts devraient toujours être placés proche des sillets. Ainsi vous obtenez le meilleur son et, cela enseigne aussi votre bras et vos doigts avec exactitude ou se trouvent les notes. C'est ici que la correcte mémoire musculaire commence Dernièrement, pendant la pratique des passages de gammes, les phalanges devraient être parallèles au manche.

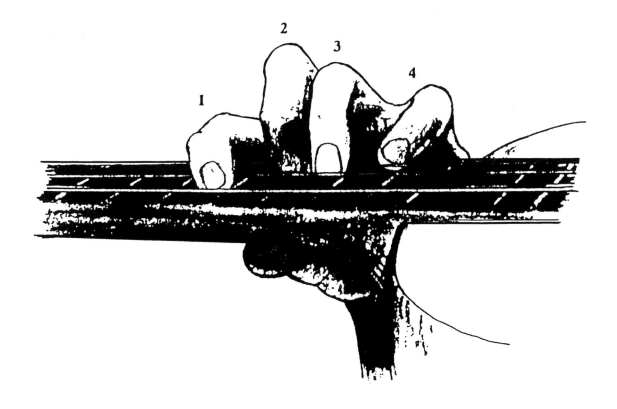

Tárrega in his later years

前書き

　アンドレス・セゴビアの夢は、主にスペインの居酒屋で民俗音楽家の手によって弾かれていたギターというものをコンサートステージに引っ張りだすことだったんだ。まず、ギターが一流楽器に属することを証明しなくてはいけない。そのためにセゴビアは大学や音楽学校にギター科を作り、自分の弟子達をそこで教える事のできる人材に育て上げる事に成功したんだ。といってもそれは、長い下積み生活と数多くのコンサートキャリアによるセゴビアの努力の末の話だけれども。今日ギターがあるということは、本当にセゴビアの熱い夢のおかげなんだよ。ブラボー、大音楽家セゴビア！

　その昔、僕もセゴビアの下でクラッシックギターを学ぶためにスペインへ渡ったわけなんだけど、以前の僕の音楽家としてのキャリアは、スペインの居酒屋で弾いていた民俗ギタリストと同様、マイアミのナイトクラブでロックミュージシャンとして始まったんだ。それにもかかわらず、セゴビアは僕の才能を認めてくれて、自分の財布を開き、奨学金までだしてくれたよ。現在僕は、クラッシックギタリストとして、コンサートステージの上で何度もオーケストラと共演してきたし、大学で教えることのできる身分でもある。これも全てセゴビアのおかげだってこと、心から感じているよ。

　実のはなし僕の本当の夢は、セゴビアと正反対。クラッシックギターが世の中に出回るためには、もう一度、一般庶民の手に戻してやらなくてはいけない気がするんだ。そうすることによって、全てのギタリスト（ジャンル、また経験の深い浅いを問わず）にクラッシックギターの曲とテクニックに親しんでもらいたいんだ。まずそのために僕は、練習そのもの自体を、難しい理屈抜きの、シンプルで楽しいものにすることに決めたんだ。１９８０年代の中頃、「ロックギタリストのためのクラッシックギター」というタイトルの本の製作及び出版に成功して、僕の夢が現実に一歩近づいたんだよ。その本は、ノーテイションとタブ譜とテープのついた最初のクラッシックギターの教本だったんだよ。何でロック界を選んだかって？当時、僕の所に本気でクラッシックギターを習いに来た生徒のほとんどがロックギタリストだったからさ。僕も元ロックミュージシャンだから、けして驚くべきことじゃないけど。実際、少しでも多くのギタリストがクラッシックギターに親しむ様になれば、もっとたくさんの人達に真のギターの美しさを聞いて楽しんでもらうことができると思うんだ。僕の最初の本の出版から今日に至るまで、何と数千人もの新しいクラッシックギタリストが育ってきているんだよ。

　僕の書いている全部の教本は、ノーテイションとタブ譜とテープ付きなんだ。テープを聴けば、僕の編曲がいかにもギターらしく聞こえるかが分かってもらえると思うよ。後期の作曲家達は、演奏家としても優れていて自作の曲を弾くことぐらいは当たり前の話だったんだ。実のところ、あの偉大なるクラッシック曲の数々も、タブ譜とテープがあれば結構簡単に弾けちゃうってことを君達に分かってもらいたいんだ。

　　　　ベン・ボルト

筆者について

　ベン・ボルトは革命的な練習方法を用いたビデオと本の出版を通して、数千人の人々にクラッシックギターを紹介した第一人者として今日の世に認められている。以前の生徒たちは、レッスンを始めると同時に楽譜の読み方を習わなくてはいけないという、ギターに限り大変複雑な練習方法に苦しんでいた。今日、ボルトの出版により、初心者でもクラッシックギターをすぐに弾き始めるということが可能になった。線と数字の記号によって音譜を表すタブ譜と、リズム（音の長さ）を直接説明しているテープにより、誰でもクラッシックギターを弾くことができるようになっている。このボルトのアイディアは、今日の数多くの音楽出版社に真似られている事はいうまでもない。すべての音楽家にクラッシックギターに親しんでもらいたいというボルトの夢が、実現されつつある事は確かだ。

　クラッシックギターの父として知られるアンドレス・セゴビアは、次のようなコメントを残している。「ベン・ボルトは、洗練された音で弾く優秀なギタリストだ。」　実際セゴビアは、自分で開いたミュージカ・エン・コンポステラ（音楽学校）において、ベン・ボルトの教育費を負担していた。

　その昔、スペイン内乱、また第2次世界大戦中、セゴビアは母国スペインを離れ、南米ウルグアイのモンテビデオにおいて最も優秀な生徒として知られるアベル・カルレバロの教育に10年間の月日を費やしていた。同時にセゴビアは戦争の火花の飛び交うヨーロッパでは全くコンサートを行っていなかったといわれている。この歴史的事実に目を付けたベン・ボルトは、当時アベル・カルレバロが教えていたフランスのパリへ足を運び、彼の下でさらにセゴビア流クラッシックギターを学ぶ。次にカルレバロの勧めによりベン・ボルトは全額援助の上で、ブラジル・インターナショナル・ギター学院でカルレバロ教育を受け続ける。そこでは、セゴビア流、またカルレバロ流技術を学ぶことになる。次の数年間ベン・ボルトは、カルレバロの故郷、ウルグアイのモンテビデオにおいて、カルレバロ、そしてイタリアの有名作曲家兼指揮者ガイド・サントルソラのもとで最後の音楽教育を終了している。

　ベン・ボルトの書いている数冊の本はベストセラー・リストに含まれていて、ビデオ「Anyone Can Play the Classic Guitar」は大学レベルのクラッシックギター教育におき、参考資料として扱われてもいる。また、ベン・ボトは数百万本を売り続けているメルベイ出版のビデオ「Modern Guitar Method Book I」などにも登場している。

　ベン・ボルトの日々の生活は、本の出版、オーケストラとの共演、そして大学レベルでの教育とに分けられている。ベン・ボルトは次の三点がそろうとき、誰でもクラッシックギターを上手に弾くことができると信じている。1、良い楽器　2、良い教師　3、興味をそそる音楽：

　ベン・ボルトの出版物はカリフォルニアで毎年行われている、NAMMショー（ナショナル・アソシエーション・オブ・ミュージック・マーチェント）そしてドイツのインターナショナルNAMMショーなどによって取り上げられてもいる。

Toll Free 1-800-8-MEL BAY (1-800-863-5229) FAX 314-257-5062

他の本
by
Ben Bolt

ノーテイションとタブ譜付き。ブルーススケール、オクターブ、ペンタトニックスケール、ダブルストップ、コードそしてアルペジオなどの練習。コードやスケールの種明かし。そして音楽理論や和音などの正しい使い方など。本$4．95．テープ$9．98．

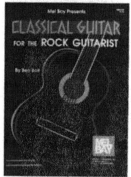

最近のロックミュージシャンは、あらゆる角度からの音楽の習得によりロック界の国境を広げている。この教本は、ロックギターとクラッシックギターを知り尽くしたベン・ボルトによって書かれていて、分かり安さを追求した教えのなかで、クラッシックギターパフォーマンス、ミュージシャンシップ、フレージングなどの基礎が説明されている。選曲は、パコベルのキャノン、グリーグのアニトラズ・ダンス、ラベルのパバン・フォー・ア・デッド・チャイルド、サティのジムノペディそしてモーツァルトのロンド・アラ・トルカ（ほか多数）などで、楽しさをモットーとしたベン・ボルトによる編曲。タブ譜とノーテーション付き。本$6．95．テープ$9．98．ビデオ $24．95．

音譜読みは、壮大で刺激的な音楽の世界の扉を開くカギでもある。この教本の中では、普通とは違ったユニークな音譜読み習得法が説明されていてる。筆者は、言う。「もし今までに、楽譜を読む事の難しさにいらだった人がいたら、この本は、きっとそんな人のためになるよ。」タブ譜とノーテーション付き。本$5．95．テープ$9．98．

アメリカの有名ティーチャー　ベン・ボルトによる分かり安さを追求したクラッシックギターの教え。右手の無駄のない指の動き、両手の位置そしてギターを弾く時の正しい姿勢などの説明。45分　ビデオ　$24．95．

ギターリスト　ベン・ボルトの編曲による人気クラッシックの15曲。何世紀も前のルート曲なども含まれている。クラッシックギターandスティールギター用。タブ譜とノーテーション付き。本$7．95．テープ$9．98．ビデオ$24．95．

フランシスコ・タルレガ

　１８５２年１１月２１日、スペインのビニャリアルに生まれたフランシスコ・タルレガは、後のギター音楽界に最大の影響を与えた作曲家ギタリストである。少年タルレガは、当時の人気ギタリスト、マニュエル・ゴンサレスの演奏にすっかり聞き入ってしまい、１１歳にして最初のレッスンを彼より受ける。その後フェリックス・ポンサからも習っている。

　まだ幼かった頃タルレガは、ある事故により命は取り止めたものの、両目の視力を大幅に減少させてしまい、痛々しくも回復の困難な眼炎という結果を招いてしまう。結局この幼時の暗い記憶が少人数あいてのコンサートだけしか好まなかった晩年の内気なタルレガの性格を築きあげていった。

　マドリッド音楽院にてハーモニー、ソルフェイジ、ピアノそして作曲などの基礎教育を終了したタルレガは、１８７５年、２３歳の若さでハーモニーと作曲のコンクールにおき優勝している。１８８０年、２９歳のときタルレガがフランスのパリで行ったコンサートは、かなりの熱狂ぶりだった。その後ヨーロッパ各地で行ったコンサートのほとんどが成功に終わっている。

　ロマン派スタイルや独特なフィンガーリングなどを含めた楽器の十分な理解より、タルレガはギターの可能性を大幅に広げてしまった。だから今日のクラッシックギタリストのほとんどが彼の影響下にあるということが出来よう。

　タルレガは１９０９年１２月１５日に、バルセロナにて死去している。１９１６年、故郷のビニャリアルにタルレガの思い出と共に記念碑がたてられる。そこには次のような言葉が残されている。

　　　１８５２年１１月２１日、偉大なるギタリストこの家に生まれる。
　　　ビニャリアルの名誉と栄光、フランシスコ・タルレガ。

　今日でもスペインでは街の小道の数本にタルレガの名が付けられていて、あたたかく又素朴に生きた天才タルレガを讃えている。

　　　　　　　　　　　　　　　ベン・ボルト

タブ譜
（タブ）
タブ譜は、古来の楽譜だけど、簡単に読めるから今日でも使われている。

タブは、6本の線上に書かれているんだ。この6本の線は、ギターの6本の弦を表している。

```
     1st ──────────────────────────────
弦   2nd ──────────────────────────────
     3rd ──────────────────────────────
     4th ──────────────────────────────
     5th ──────────────────────────────
     6th ──────────────────────────────
```

下の数字は、フレットの番号を表しているんだ。つまりこの場合は、1弦の1フレット、3フレット、5フレットの順で弾くことになるんだ。

```
──────────────1───3───5──────────
──────────────────────────────────
──────────────────────────────────
──────────────────────────────────
──────────────────────────────────
──────────────────────────────────
```

次に、縦に書かれた数字は、同時に弾こう。

Eコード

```
──────────────0───────────
──────────────0───────────
──────────────1───────────
──────────────2───────────
──────────────2───────────
──────────────0───────────
```

楽譜

音程

音符は、5本の線の上に書かれる。これを **五線** と呼ぶ。音符は、線上または、線と線の間にかかれるんだ。

五線内では表せない高い音または、低いおとは、**加線** によって表すことができる。

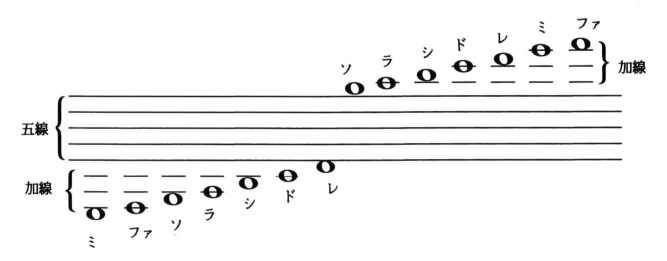

日本の ド レ ミ ファ ソ ラ シ ド は、英語では、C D E F G A B C。 ドからド、レからレなどを **1オクターブ** と呼ぶんだ。

1オクターブ　ド レ ミ ファ ソ ラ シ ド

どの五線も最初に **音部記号** がついているんだ。ギターの楽譜は、ト音記号を使うんだ。

音部記号
（ト音記号）

シャープ　フラット　ナチュラル
（臨時記号）

　シャープ　フラット　ナチュラル　は、1フレット分の音を上げたり下げたりするもの。ギターの1フレットは、半音に値するんだ。シャープ　フラット　ナチュラルには、それぞれの記号があって、音符の前に付けられるんだよ。

　　　シャープ　　♯　　1フレット（半音）上がる。

　　　フラット　　♭　　1フレット（半音）下がる。

　　　ナチュラル　♮　　シャープやフラットの付いた音符をしらふにする（元の音に戻す）。

音符の形は、その音の長さ表すんだ。

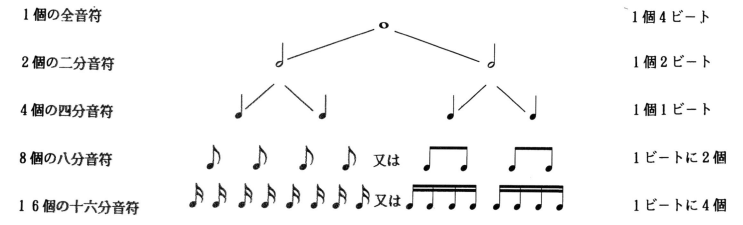

1個の全音符	1個4ビート
2個の二分音符	1個2ビート
4個の四分音符	1個1ビート
8個の八分音符	1ビートに2個
16個の十六分音符	1ビートに4個

休符

　それぞれの音符に値する休符（鳴らない音）があるんだ。

全休符	二分休符	四分休符	八分休符	十六分休符

　音譜は、数学的に縦線によって作られる小節によって区切られているんだ。それぞれの小節内のビート数は、音部記号の次に書かれている拍子記号によって決められるんだ。

　　　拍子記号　　$\frac{2}{4}$　　$\frac{3}{4}$　　$\frac{4}{4}$　　$\frac{3}{8}$　　$\frac{6}{8}$　　etc.

　上の数字は、小節内のビートの数を表し、下の数字は、どの音符が1ビートに値するかを表している。

$$\frac{3}{4} \quad = \quad 1小節 = 3ビート$$
= 1ビート＝四分音符
= 2つの八分音符
= 4つの十六分音符

一番よく使われる拍子記号は、 $\frac{4}{4}$ で **C** とも書かれることがある。

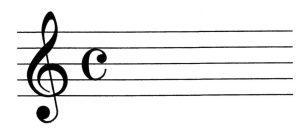

調号

ある曲がどの調（音階）に属するかを決めるためには、**調号**が用いられる。調号は、最初の小節のあたまにまとまって現れるシャープ又は、フラットの固まりを示す。

この場合、1曲を通してすべてのファにシャープが付くことになる。

付点音符

付点は、音符の右側につき、その音符の長さを2分の3倍にする。
(1.5倍)

付点休符

付点が右側に付き2分の3の休符になる。

ダブルシャープ

ダブルシャープの付いた音符は、1音（2フレット）上げる。例えば、ソにダブルシャープが付くと2フレット上げてラになる。

記号は、これ ✖

46

ダブルフラット

ダブルフラットの付いた音符は、1音（2フレット）下げる。ミにダブルフラットが付くとレになる。

記号は、これ　　　♭♭

反復記号　（リピート）

 前にあるものを繰り返す。

 後に来るものを繰り返す。

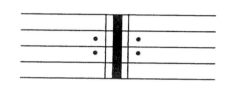 前にあるものを繰り返したら、次に後に来るものを繰り返す。

右手

フィンガーリング　（ピッキング）

日本語	英語	スペイン語	シンボル
親指	Thumb	Pulgar	p
人指し指	Index	Indice	i
中指	Middle	Medio	m
薬指	Ring	Anular	a

ポジション　（位置）

親指（p）　人指し指（i）　中指（m）　薬指（a）の順でギターの3弦の上におくのがベスト。（図を見よう）

47

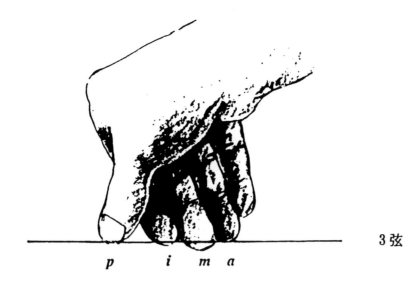

3弦

p i m a

ストロークの練習

　pを使うレスト・ストローク：まずaを1弦、mを2弦、iを3弦に置き、pで6弦を
ゆっくり滑らすように弾く。その際、pが下の5弦で止まるまで弾き下ろす。全部の
ベース弦（4、5、6弦）で練習しよう。

　i，m，aを使うレスト・ストローク：pを6弦に置き、iで3弦をゆっくり滑らすよ
うに弾く。その祭、iが上の4弦で止まるまで弾き上げる。同じ事を、mで2弦、aで
1弦でやってみよう。弦を弾く指の1番先の関節を曲げないで弾く。また、iとm、i
とa、mとaの組み合わせで連続したレスト・ストロークの練習をトレブル弦（1、2、
3弦）を使ってやってみよう。僕の場合、人指し指と薬指が同じ長さだからiとaの組み
合わせを良く使うんだ。

　フリー・ストローク：弦を弾いた指がほかの弦で止まらない弾き方。指の1番先の関節
は曲げる。ただし、この場合ロックベースのチョッパー奏法みたいに弦をひっかき上げな
いように注意しよう。

　どのストロークの時でも、爪と指の先端の皮膚が同時に弦をかするように弾くのが
1番きれいな音をだすコツ！

左手

フィンガーリング

人指し指　＝　1
中指　　　＝　2
薬指　　　＝　3
小指　　　＝　4

ポジション

　左手については、曲によっていろいろな動きをするから、一言では説明ができないんだ。だけど、つぎの四つの基本をいつでも忘れないようにしよう。

1．爪はギターのフィンガーボードに触れないように、いつも短くしておく。
2．親指はネックの裏側の中心、反対側からみた人指し指と中指の真ん中辺に位置させよう。（図を見よう。）
3．指はいつでもフレットのすぐ後ろで弦をおさえる。そうすれば、一番良い音が出るし、また腕と指にフレット探しにおいて理想的な癖がつくんだ。
4．スケールを弾く時は、指の関節がフィンガーボードと平行になるように。

訳　木村友紀
Translation : Tomo Kimura

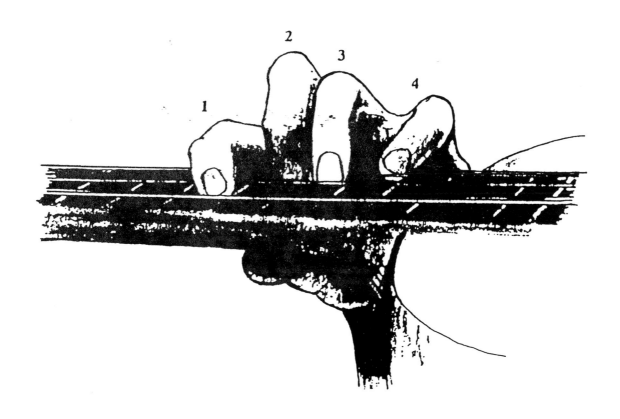

49

PRELUDE IN E

Ed. Ben Bolt

Francisco Tárrega
(1852–1902)

PRELUDE IN A MINOR

Ed. Ben Bolt

F. Tárrega

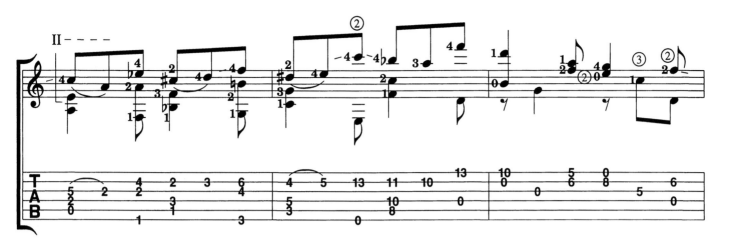

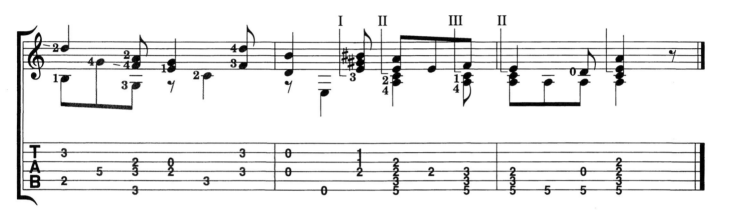

LÁGRIMA
(Prelude)

Ed. Ben Bolt

F. Tárrega

PRELUDE IN G MAJOR

Ed. Ben Bolt

F. Tárrega

PRELUDE IN D MAJOR

Ed. Ben Bolt

F. Tárrega

A sketch of Tárrega drawn by Miguel Llobet. The story goes that while in Paris Llobet drew this caricature from memory.

PRELUDE IN D MINOR

Ed. Ben Bolt

Francisco Tárrega

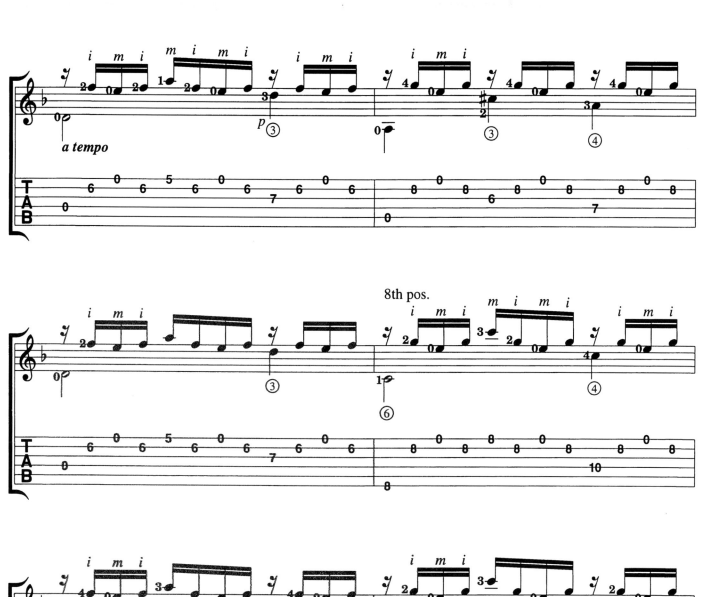

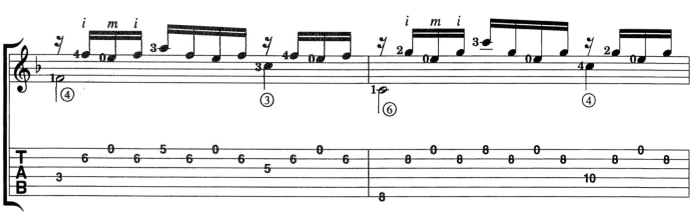

PRELUDE IN D

Ed. Ben Bolt

F. Tárrega

⑥ = D(Re)

PRELUDE

(Endecha)

Ed. Ben Bolt

⑥ = D(Re)

F. Tárrega

PRELUDE
(Lento)

Ed. Ben Bolt

F. Tárrega

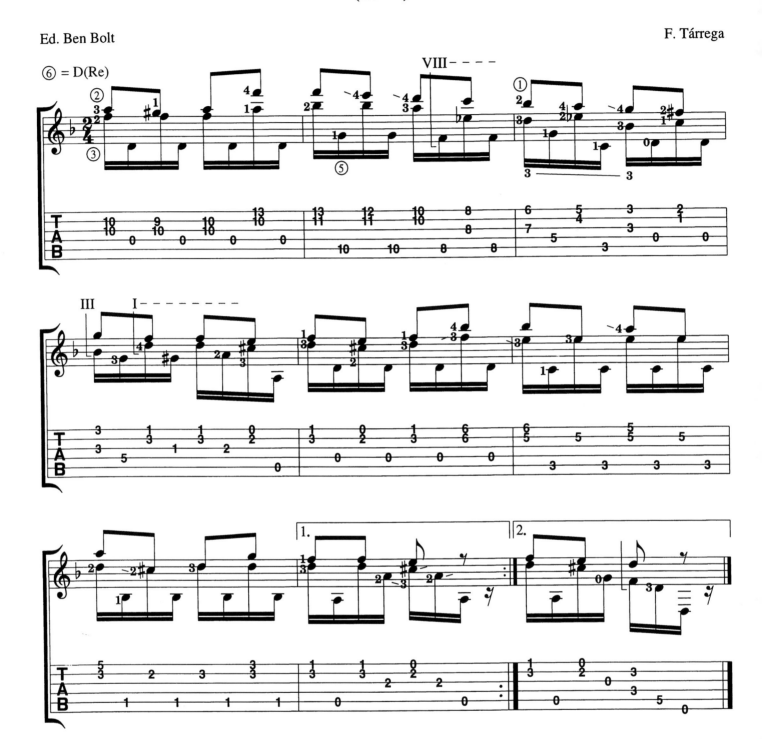

Ben Bolt
"Ben plays with a lot of feeling."
—Andres Segovia

PRELUDE
(Moderato)

Ed. Ben Bolt

F. Tárrega

⑥ = D(Re)

Moderato

PRELUDE

Ed. Ben Bolt

F. Tárrega

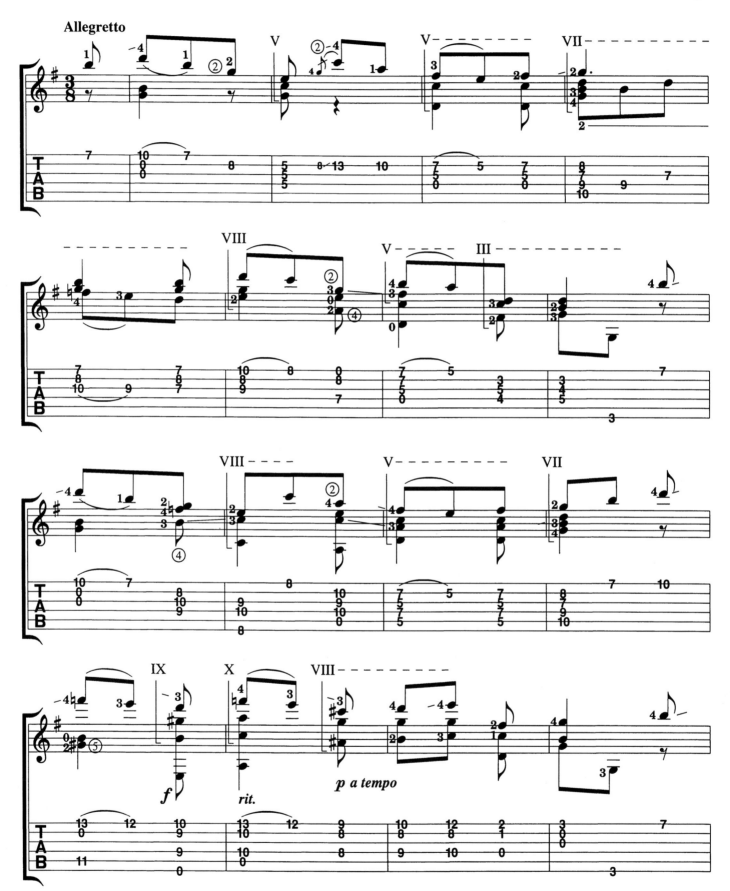

69

PRELUDE

Ed. Ben Bolt

F. Tárrega

PRELUDE IN A

Ed. Ben Bolt

F. Tárrega

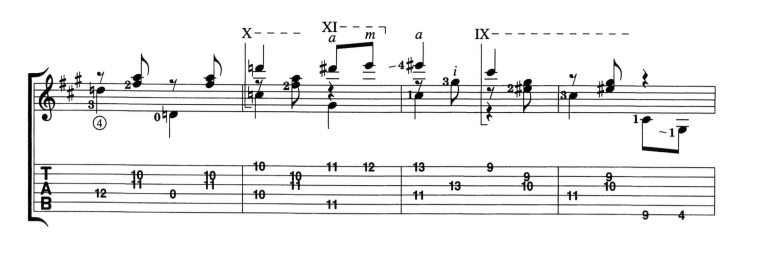

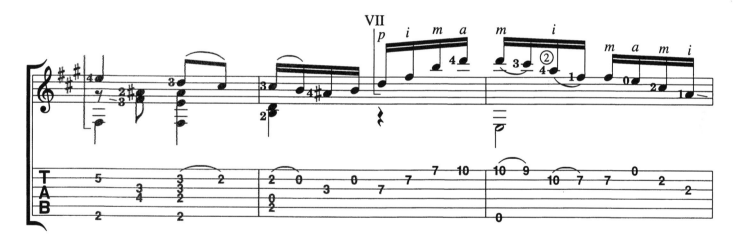

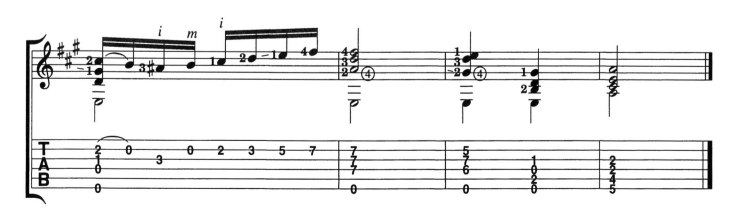

PRELUDE IN A MINOR

Ed. Ben Bolt

F. Tárrega

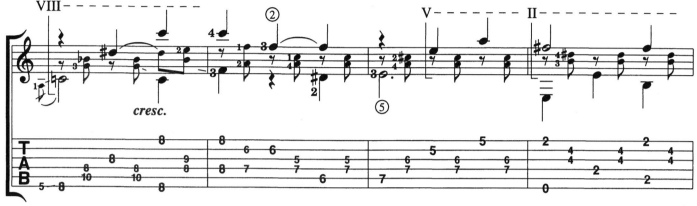

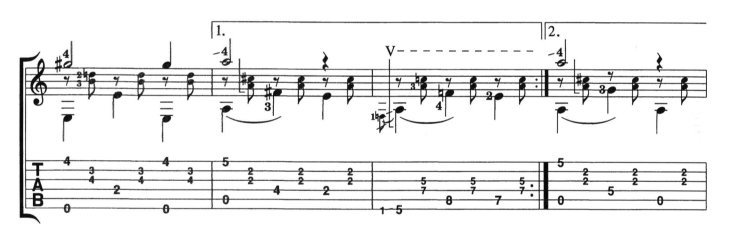

PRELUDE

Ed. Ben Bolt

F. Tárrega

PRELUDE

Ed. Ben Bolt

F. Tárrega

PRELUDE IN A MAJOR

Ed. Ben Bolt

Francisco Tarrega

DANZA MORA

Ed. Ben Bolt

F. Tárrega

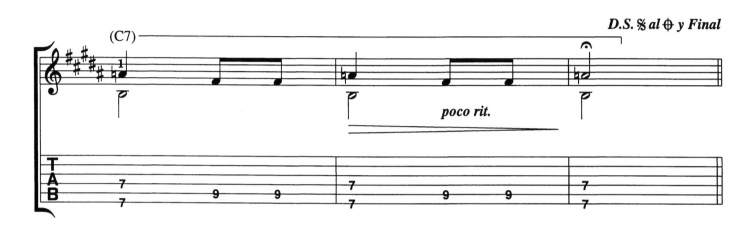

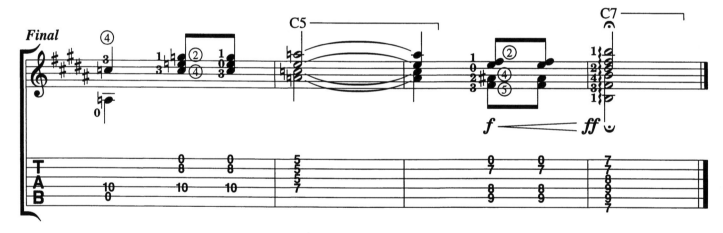

¡MARIETA!

Mazurca

Ed. Ben Bolt

F. Tárrega

MAZURCA EN SOL

A mi querido amigo el eminente oculista Dr. Dn. SANTIAGO ALBIROS

Ed. Ben Bolt

F. Tárrega

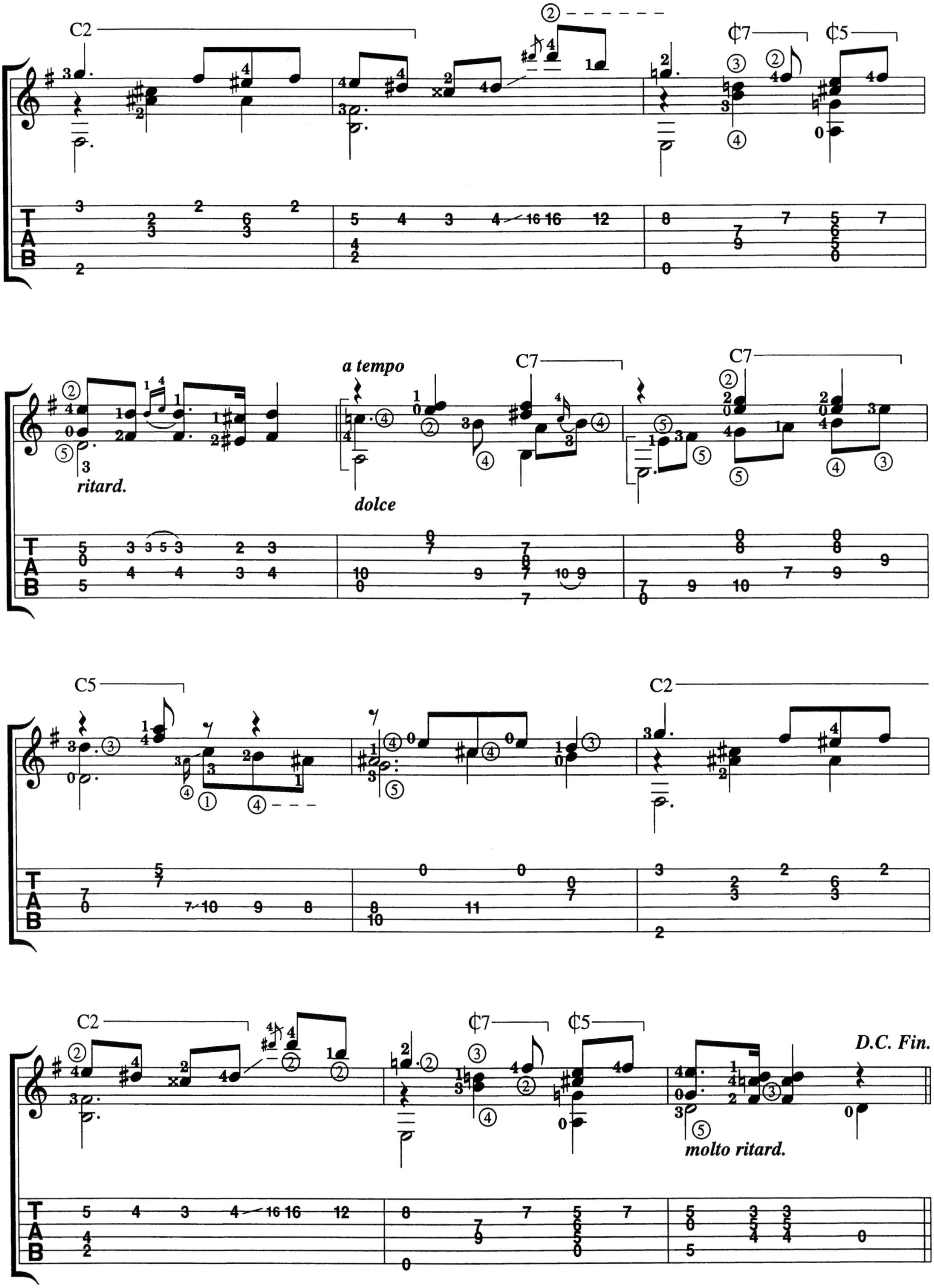
C2
₵7
₵5
ritard.
a tempo
C7
dolce
C7
C5
C2
C2
₵7
₵5
molto ritard.
D.C. Fin.

MARIA

Gavota

A mi querido amigo, el eminente mandolinista, D. BALDOMERO CATEURA.

Ed. Ben Bolt

F. Tárrega

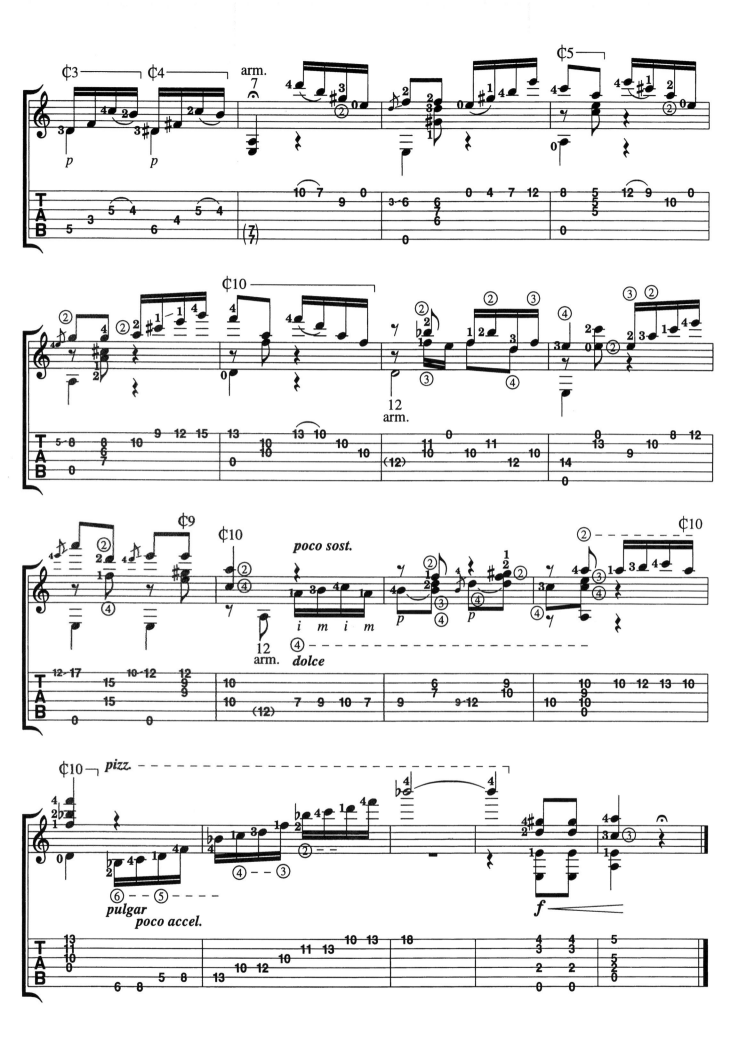

MINUETTO

A mi predilecta discipula y noble Srta. Maria Rita Brondi

Ed. Ben Bolt

F. Tárrega

ADELITA
Mazurca

Ed. Ben Bolt

F. Tárrega

PAVANA

Ed. Ben Bolt

F. Tárrega

LA ALBORADA

Cajita de Música

A mi hijo Paquito

Ed. Ben Bolt

F. Tárrega

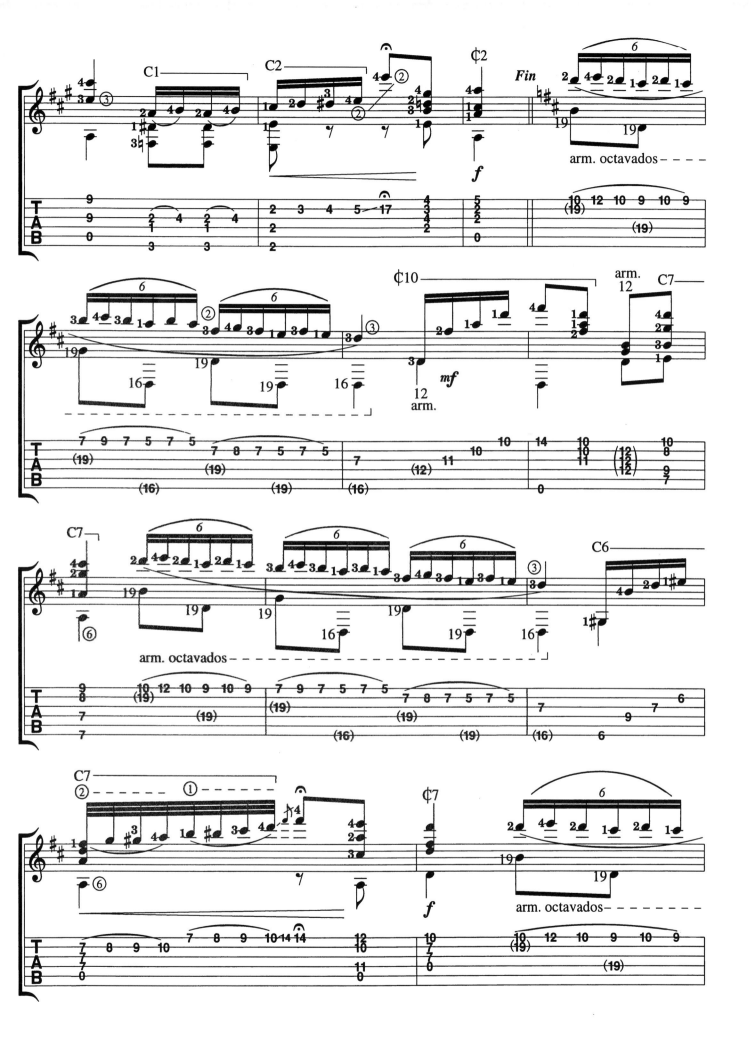

103

CAPRICHO ARABE
Serenata

Ed. Ben Bolt

F. Tárrega

105

THE BUTTERFLY
(La Mariposa)

Ed. Ben Bolt

Francisco Tárrega

Tune 6th string down to D.

Allegretto

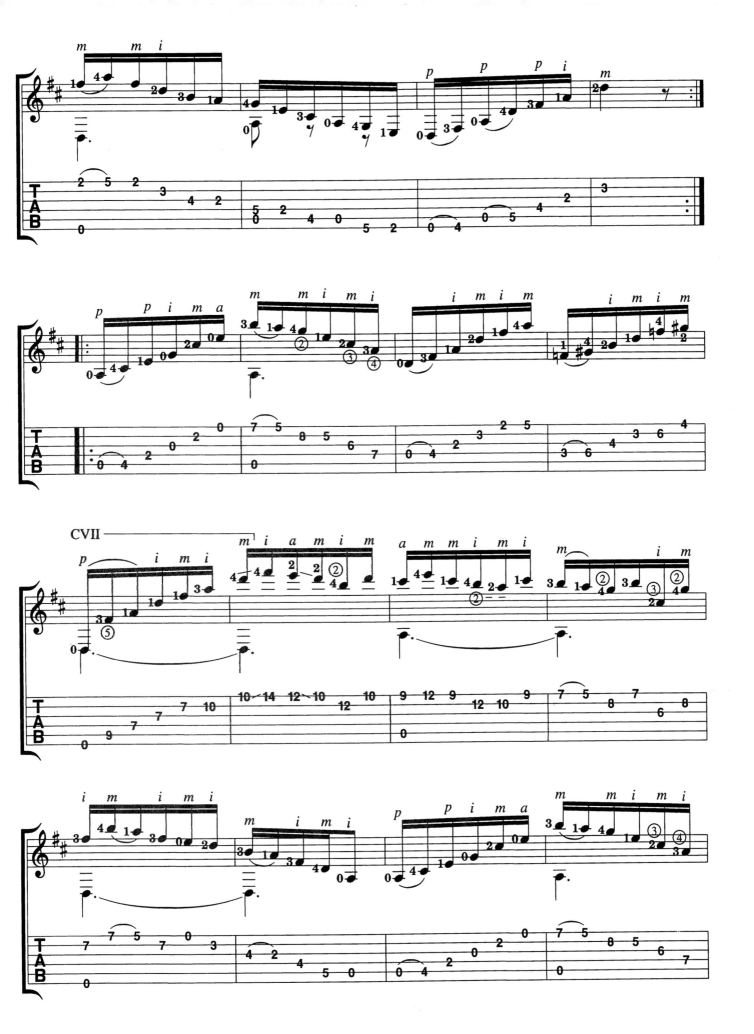

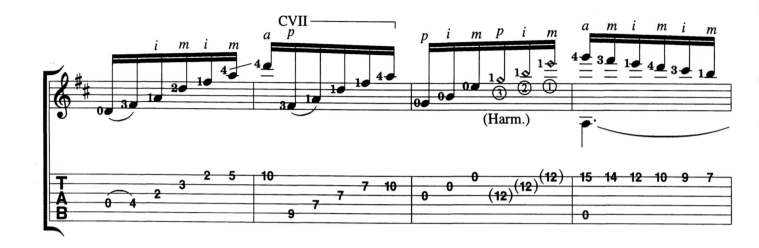

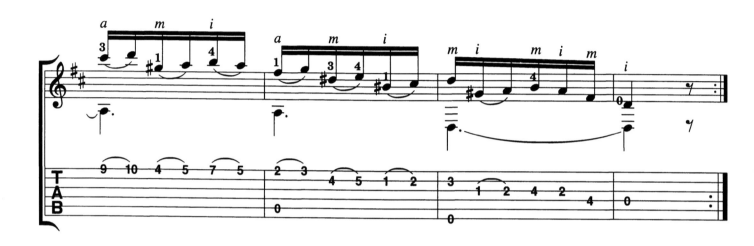

ROSITA

Ed. Ben Bolt

F. Tárrega

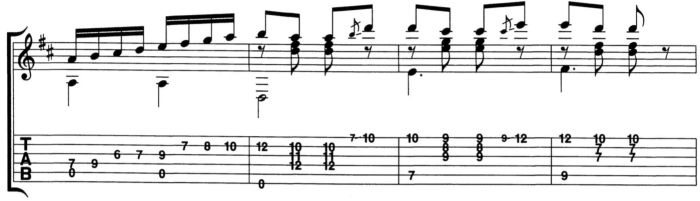

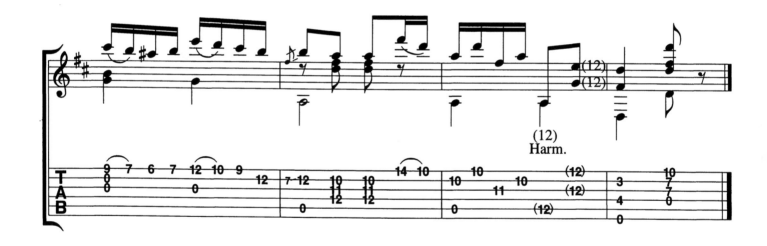

RECUERDOS DE LA ALHAMBRA

Homenaje al eminente artista, ALFREDO COTTIN.

Ed. Ben Bolt

F. Tárrega

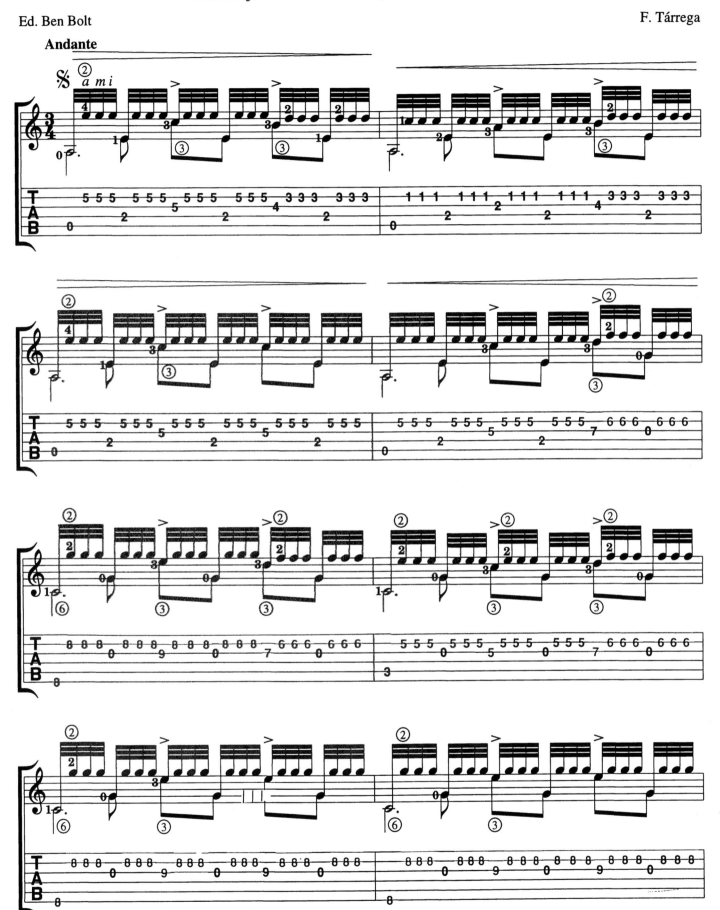

119

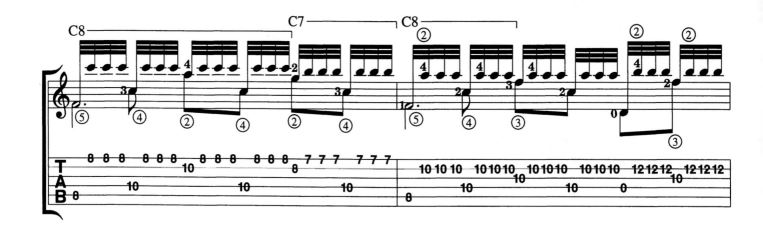

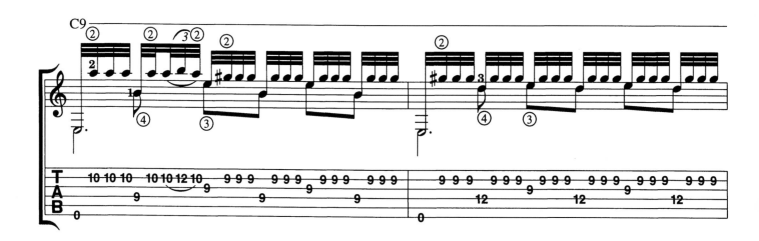

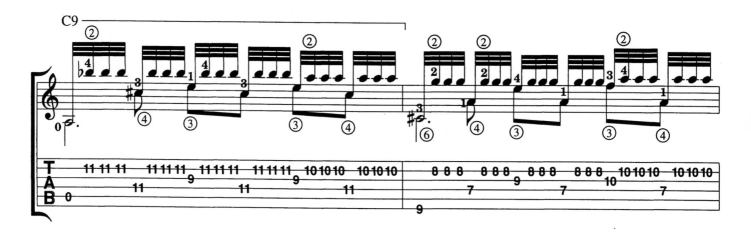

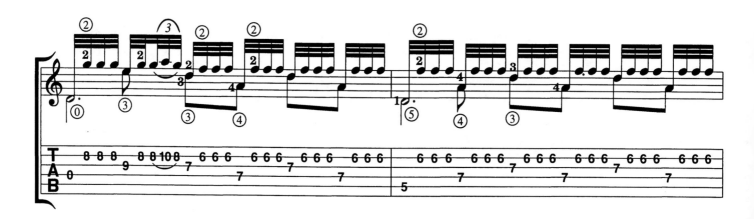

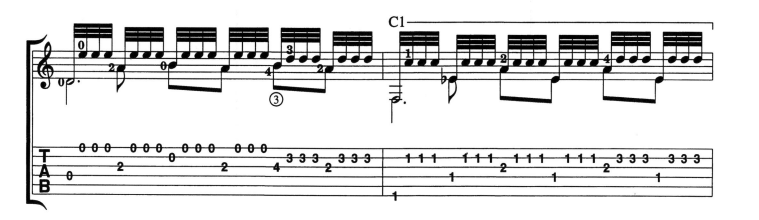

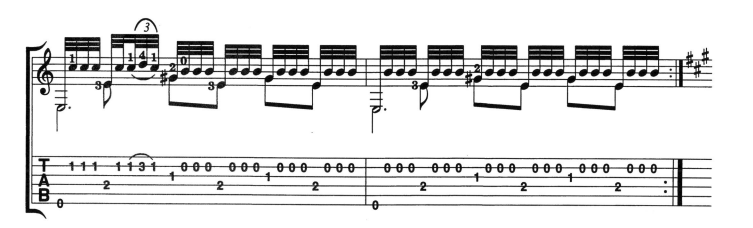

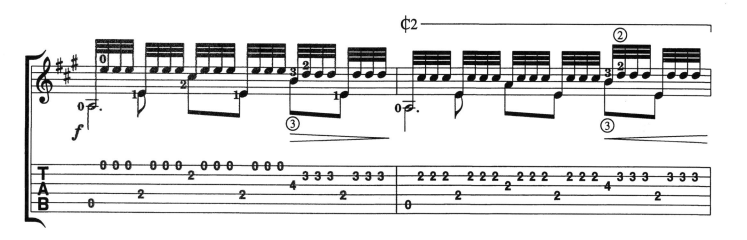

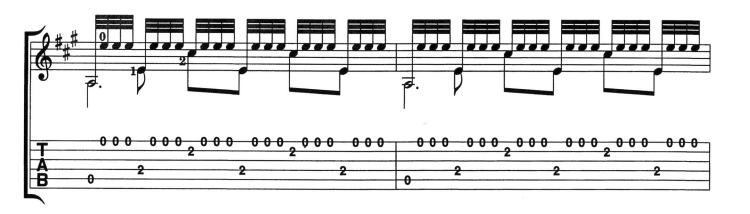

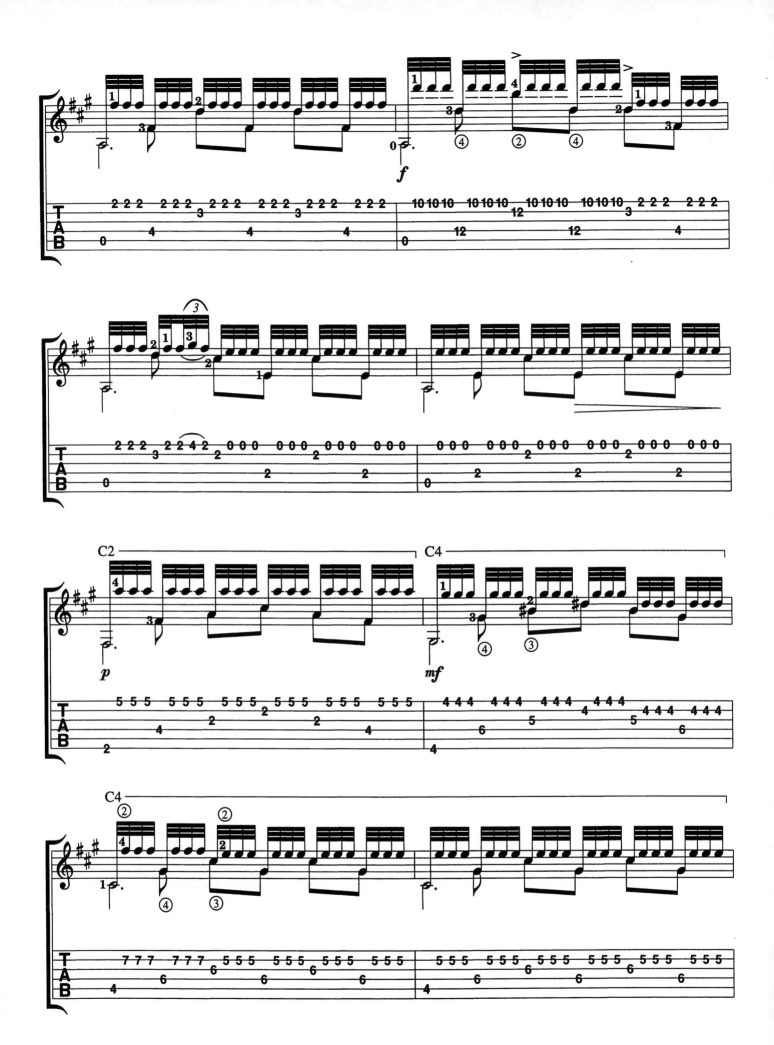

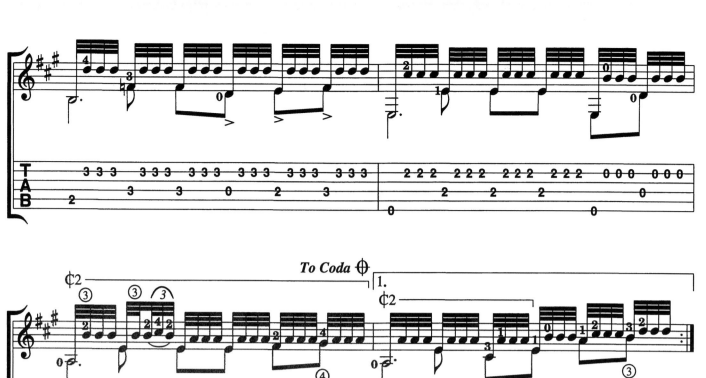

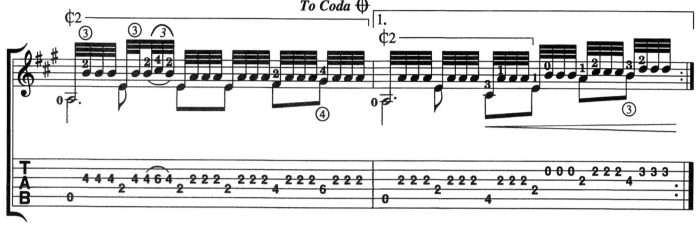

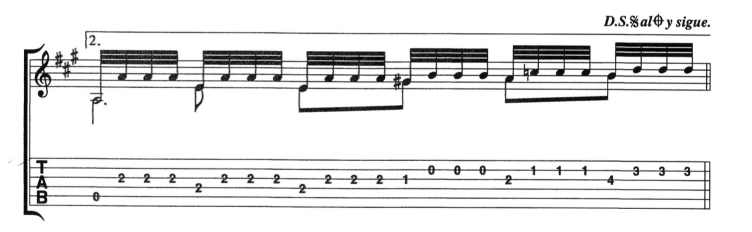

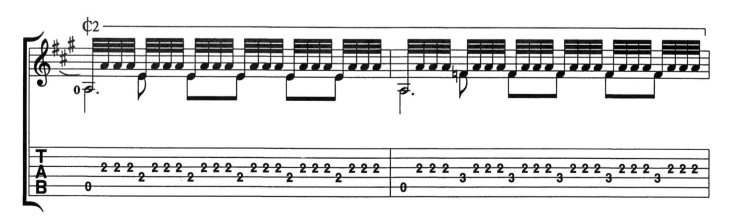

123

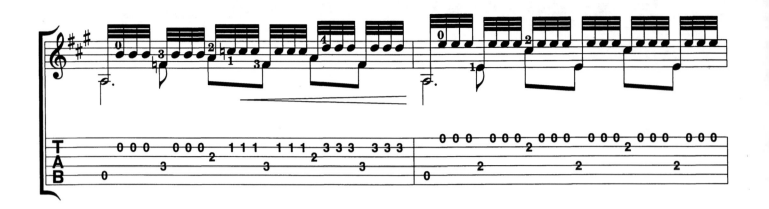

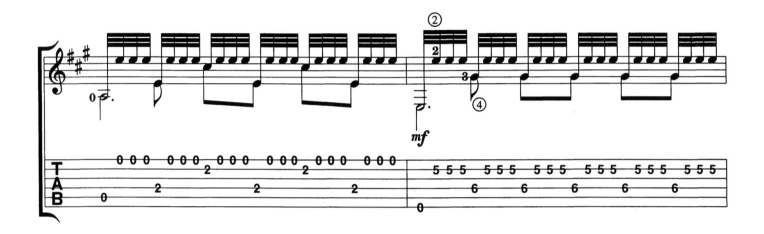

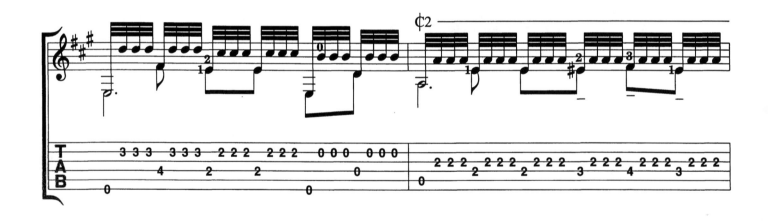

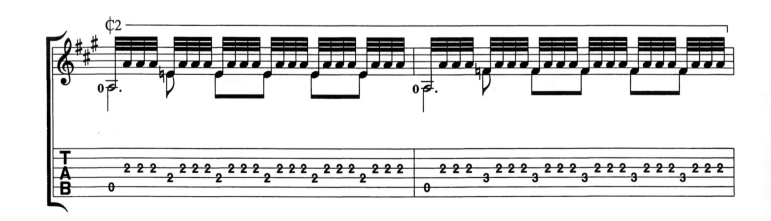

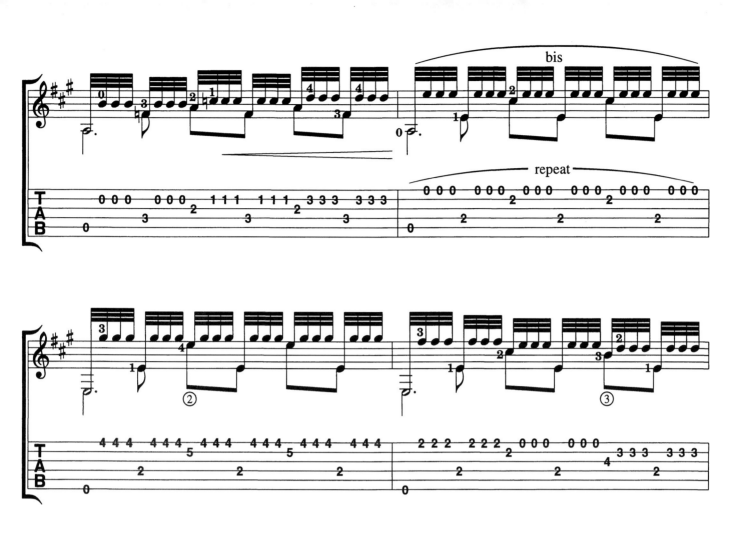

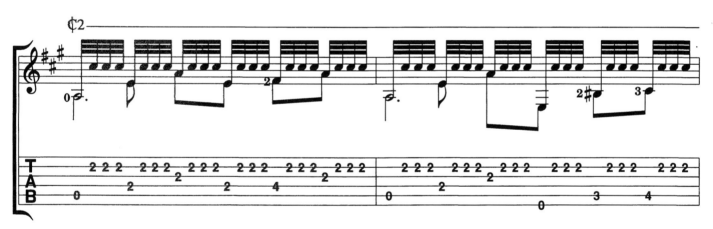

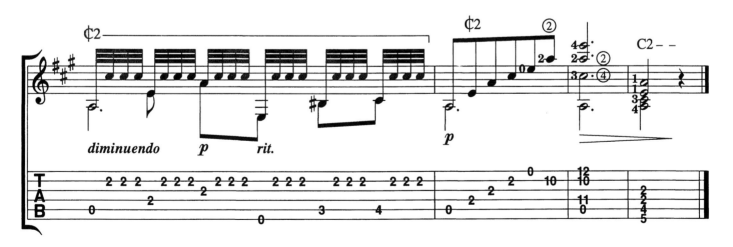

Great Music at Your Fingertips